A Night in Provence

A Comedy

by Robin Hawdon

A SAMUEL FRENCH ACTING EDITION

SAMUEL FRENCH

FOUNDED 1830

NEW YORK HOLLYWOOD LONDON TORONTO

SAMUELFRENCH.COM

IMPORTANT BILLING AND CREDIT REQUIREMENTS

All producers of *A NIGHT IN PROVENCE must* give credit to the Author of the Play in all programs distributed in connection with performances of the Play, and in all instances in which the title of the Play appears for the purposes of advertising, publicizing or otherwise exploiting the Play and/or a production. The name of the Author *must* appear on a separate line on which no other name appears, immediately following the title and *must* appear in size of type not less than fifty percent of the size of the title type.

A NIGHT IN PROVENCE was first produced at the Mill at Sonning Dinner Theater in October 2007, directed by Ian Masters, with the following cast:

FRED..Darren Machin
JUDY...Lisa Hall
SHAUN...Toby Dale
MOIRA...Jemma Churchill
MAURICE...Michael Frenner
YVETTE...MaryConlon

CHARACTERS

FRED – a Londoner
JUDY – his wife
SHAUN – an Irishman
MOIRA – his wife
MAURICE – a Parisian
YVETTE – his wife

All are in their late thirties/early forties.

The author has no objection if American producers wish to make Shaun and Moira American or Irish-American, rather than Irish.

SETTING

The main living area of a traditional affluent holiday home in the south of France. Wide, open-plan space. Upstage center the front door with a small window to the side. Perhaps a raised entrance area. Upstage left an open plan kitchen area separated from the main room by tiled work units, and with an exit offstage left. Downstage left an arched door to the main bedroom suite. Stage right an arch to the guest bedrooms. Fireplace, large sofa centre stage, French rustic furniture.

On the forestage a terrace running the full width of the stage, accessed centre via imaginary French windows or sliding glass doors from the house. A patio couch with swing seat stands to one side, with folding patio table and chairs stacked nearby.

Light and shade and Provençal colors everywhere.

ACT ONE

(The afternoon sun is pouring in from the terrace. The sound of a car engine is heard, and doors slam. Voices are heard from outside.)

FRED. *(off)* All right, all right – I'll bring the cases, you unlock the door.

JUDY. Where's the key, Fred?

FRED. Well, I dunno! You had it.

JUDY. Here it is.

FRED. Get on with it then – we'll melt out here!

(A key rattles in the lock.)

JUDY. *(off)* It won't open.

FRED. *(off)* Turn it the other way, you silly woman.

(The front door opens. **JUDY** *enters with* **FRED** *behind dragging two large suitcases.)*

JUDY. Here we are then.

FRED. Thank Christ for that! Pfff – what the bloody hell you got in here – Marks and Sparks lingerie department?

JUDY. *(looking round)* Oo, look at this, Fred. This is nice!

FRED. *(as he dumps the cases)* Phew! *(looks round)* Yeh, not bad.

JUDY. This is classy! *(goes to the kitchen area)* En suite kitchen – very posh.

FRED. *(wiping his brow)* Gawd, it's warm.

(comes downstage to the imaginary terrace doors, opens them and gazes out front)

Oh, look at that view!

JUDY. They've got a dish-washer.

FRED. You can see the sea.

7

JUDY. They've got a lovely big fridge-freezer.

FRED. Never mind that – come and look at the view.

JUDY. *(looking in cupboards)* I wonder where they keep the pans and everything.

FRED. Never mind the bloody pans – come and look at the view!

(She comes down-stage and stares out front.)

JUDY. Oo, yes. You can see the sea.

FRED. That's what I said.

JUDY. Well, it said sea views – you jolly well ought to see it. Nice terrace. Pretty flowers.

FRED. Bogganvillyer, that is.

JUDY. Where's the pool?

FRED. Oh, yeh…*(peering off to the side)* There it is – down there.

JUDY. Oo, yes. Looks nice.

FRED. Bloody better be – the amount we're paying. You must get to it off the end of the terrace.

JUDY. Looks like one of those naked goddess statues at one end.

FRED. Oh good. Might encourage everyone else to strip off too.

JUDY. One track mind you've got, Fred. *(going back)* Nice tiles. Better than carpets – won't need to hoover.

FRED. Thank God for that.

JUDY. Let's have a look at the bathrooms.

FRED. Now one thing you're not bloody doing is spending the whole holiday in the bathroom.

JUDY. I'm just looking.

FRED. You're not doing your hair all day, you're not doing your make-up, you're not dressing up for a bloody Buckingham Palace garden party – all right?

JUDY. All right, all right, Fred. Don't go on. What's in here?

(opens the door to the main bedroom suite)

Looks like the main bedroom. Oo, it's very nice!

(goes through)

FRED. *(to himself)* Well thank God *she's* happy.

JUDY. *(off)* Oo, look at this, Fred.

FRED. *(collecting the suitcases)* Has it got an en suite bathroom? If it's en suite it's the main bedroom.

JUDY. *(off)* Oo, yes – look! Two basins, bidet and everything!

FRED. *(struggling to the bedroom with the suitcases)* Oh Lord! She'll be washing everything all day long.

JUDY. *(off)* It's got French windows onto the terrace too. Isn't that dangerous, Fred? Anyone could come in while you're asleep.

FRED. You should be so lucky. *(vanishing into the bedroom)* Oh yeh – quite nice this. We'll take this one as we're here first.

JUDY. *(off)* Put my case there. I'll start unpacking.

FRED. *(off)* Not yet, for Chrissake! We haven't seen the rest of it yet. Come and look at the rest.

JUDY. *(off)* I don't want my clothes to crease.

(He returns, and crosses to the other side.)

FRED. *(calling back)* Don't be stupid – they've already been packed two days! Now there should be two other bedrooms off here somewhere.

(goes off to the other bedroom wing)

JUDY. *(following)* Well, at least the bedrooms are separate. We won't all hear each other bonking and everything.

FRED. *(off)* Oh good. We're going to do some of that then, are we?

JUDY. *(going off)* Now, Fred...don't start.

FRED. *(off)* Oh, yes. These are all right. Nice place altogether really.

JUDY. *(off)* Don't like that colour. I couldn't sleep in there.

FRED. *(off)* What's the colour matter if you're asleep?

JUDY. *(off)* Moira wouldn't like it either. They'll want that room.

FRED. *(off)* Well, they can take their choice, can't they? They can bonk alternate nights in each one. *(reappears muttering)* Knowing them they will too. Lucky buggers!

JUDY. *(reappearing after him)* Now, Fred, don't start.

FRED. *(grabbing her round the waist)* Come on then – let's have a quick one before they arrive.

JUDY. *(pushing him away)* Get off Fred! We've only just got here!

FRED. Probably the only chance I'll get.

JUDY. Well I'm not getting all messed up for when they walk through the door.

FRED. You messed up. That'll be the day!

JUDY. Anyone'd think you were eighteen, not forty four.

FRED. Oh, sorry. No-one told me it all stopped when you reached forty.

JUDY. Fred! Come on – let's go and look at the pool.

(comes downstage, through the imaginary terrace doors)

Must be this way.

(goes offstage at the other end from the patio couch)

FRED. *(following)* 'Course we could always do it in the pool. Then you'd be bonking and washing all the same time.

(Closes the imaginary terrace doors behind him, and follows her off. Pause. The sound of another car arriving. Doors slam.)

MAURICE. *(voice off)* Qu'est ce que c'est – cette voiture?

YVETTE. *(off)* Je n'sais pas.

(A key rattles. MAURICE and YVETTE enter with light luggage.)

MAURICE. *(calling)* 'Allo? *(silence)* Personne.

YVETTE. *(coming down-stage and looking at the view)* Ahh! Voila.

MAURICE. *(looks around, tests a surface for dust)* Oui – ca va.

YVETTE. *(opens the terrace doors and sighs happily)* Chez moi!

MAURICE. *(long-suffering)* Oui, oui.

YVETTE. *(staring towards the pool)* Uh? Qui est'ce?

MAURICE. *(coming to look)* Quoi?

YVETTE. *(pointing)* Près de la piscine.

MAURICE. *(frowning)* Uh? Qui est'ce?

YVETTE. Je n'sais pas.

MAURICE. Shh! Ils reviennent.

YVETTE. *(whispering)* Qui est ce?

MAURICE. *(ditto)* Je n'sais pas.

> *(They retreat inside and wait in suspense.* **FRED** *and* **JUDY** *return along the terrace.)*

FRED. Well, we'll get in that pool. First bloody thing!

JUDY. I want to unpack first.

FRED. What for? We can go in in the nude – before the others get here.

JUDY. Fred!

FRED. Why not? It's perfectly....

> *(He stops, as they enter and see the others. The two couples stare at each other.)*

MAURICE. S'il vous plaît?

FRED. Who are you?

MAURICE. *(strong French accent)* Oo are *you*?

FRED. We're staying here. This is our place.

MAURICE. Non. Zis is *our* place.

JUDY. Your place?

YVETTE. Our place.

FRED. No, no. It's our place.

MAURICE. No, no. It's our place. It belongs with us.

FRED. Belongs to you?

MAURICE. Yes. Our house.

FRED. But we've rented it. For a holiday.

MAURICE. You rent it?

FRED. Yes.

YVETTE. You rent it?

JUDY. Yes.

MAURICE. Merde!

YVETTE. *(to MAURICE)* L'agent ne te l'as pas dit?

MAURICE. *(to FRED)* You arrange with the agent?

FRED. *(nodding)* Riviera Villas – for two weeks.

MAURICE. Merde!

YVETTE. Merde!

JUDY. Two merdes. That sounds bad, Fred.

FRED. Shh! Let's get this straight. You own this house, and you weren't expecting us to be here?

MAURICE. Yes. We come for our holiday. The house is free.

FRED. It's not free.

MAURICE. It should be free.

FRED. Shit.

MAURICE. Je suis desolé. I'm very sorry, but you must leave.

JUDY. Shit.

FRED. Oh, no. Now wait a minute. We booked this house. We've paid the rent.

MAURICE. When?

FRED. Last week. Last minute booking admittedly, but we paid everything up front. The agent should have told you.

MAURICE. When you pay?

FRED. I told you, last week. Bank transfer.

JUDY. We picked up the keys in the village. It was all arranged!

YVETTE. *(sotto voce)* Maurice – as tu renseigné l'agent que nous arrivions?

FRED. What? What she say?

YVETTE. Eh? Maurice?

MAURICE. Merde!

FRED. Stop saying merde. What is it?

JUDY. They never told the agent they were coming.

FRED. *(to* MAURICE*)* That true?

(silence)

You didn't consult the agent?

(silence)

Ah, well...I'm very sorry, but that's not our fault. We made a *(French accent)* – *legitimate reservation.* It took us a hell of a time to find this place. I'm afraid there's nothing we can do about it now.

MAURICE. Ah, non. I'm desolated for the mistake, but... you will have to find somewhere else.

FRED. Are you kidding? It's high season, middle of August! Finding somewhere like this round here's impossible!

MAURICE. Yes, but er....

FRED. No way, chum! We booked and paid for this. We're staying. This is our summer holiday.

MAURICE. We too.

FRED. Well that's your problem. If this is your place, you can come any time.

MAURICE. No, no. My business, it's...impossible.

YVETTE. Impossible.

JUDY. Where are you from?

YVETTE. Paris.

FRED. Paris? Ah well, it's hardly Tooting High Street, is it? You can have a nice holiday at home anyway.

YVETTE. No, no.

MAURICE. No! Absolutely not! I'm extremely sorry for this mistake, but this is our house and we must stay here. I'm sure we can find you a nice hotel, and....

FRED. No, chum, no, sorry, but we're not going to any hotel. It's a villa we wanted – nice and private – swimming pool – near the sea. It took me bloody hours to track this down – on the internet, on the phone, trawling through the bloody adverts...There is no way we are leaving here. Got it?

YVETTE. Ah!

FRED. I'm very sorry, but if you and your agents have cocked it up between you, then it's your responsibility. You'll just have to work it out between you. We're staying. We're legally entitled.

MAURICE. Merde!

YVETTE. Je n'quitte pas, Maurice.

MAURICE. Shh!

YVETTE. Je n'quitte pas.

FRED. What she say?

JUDY. She's not going.

FRED. Now look here...I don't want to be nasty about this. I'm very sorry for the balls-up...I mean the mistake. But it's not our fault. We've driven all through France and half round bloody Provence trying to find the place – there is no way we are going to leave. D'you understand?

MAURICE. But, we...

FRED. You'll just have to tell your agents to find you somewhere else.

MAURICE. We can't go somewhere else! It's our home! We have everything here!

FRED. We've got everything here too. I had a job stopping her bringing the bloody washing machine!

YVETTE. *(fierce whisper)* Fais quelque chose, Maurice.

MAURICE. *(turning the charm onto* **JUDY***)* Madame – you can understand. The agents will find for you another place, I'm sure, but this is our home.

JUDY. Well...

FRED. No. No way. We're not leaving.

JUDY. It's very difficult.

MAURICE. Ah, mon dieu! *(to* **YVETTE***)* Qu'est ce qu'on va faire?

YVETTE. *(emphatic)* Je ne quitte pas.

FRED. She ne quittes pas, we ne quitte pas. What we going to do – fight the Battle of Waterloo?

MAURICE. You British are very...how you say? – stubborn.

FRED. Oh thanks. You make a cock-up, and we're the ones who are stubborn. You sound like Charles de Gaulle all over again.

MAURICE. I think I rather be Charles de Gaulle than Maggie Thatcher.

FRED. Oh really? And what about Jacques Chirac?

MAURICE. Nicolas Sarcozy.

FRED. Yeh – her too. I suppose. . .

JUDY. Fred! For God's sake, are we going to fight about the whole of French history?

FRED. Well...

JUDY. What are we going to *do*?

FRED. *(sitting determinedly on the sofa)* I know what I'm going to do. I'm sitting here until they take their stuff and move out, that's what I'm doing.

MAURICE. Ah, mon Dieu! *(gestures to* **YVETTE***)* Yvette.

(leads her upstage and they mutter fiercely together)

JUDY. This is just awful, Fred.

FRED. It's their problem.

JUDY. It's embarrassing! *(looking at them)* What they up to?

FRED. I dunno, but it won't work.

JUDY. He's rather dishy, isn't he?

FRED. You what?

JUDY. Well....

FRED. I don't believe this!

JUDY. I'm only saying, Fred. He's got that French charm.

FRED. I'll shove his French charm up his French arse if he doesn't get out of here.

JUDY. It is their house.

FRED. So what? They let it out, and we've rented it. We're paying them a lot of dosh for this, let me remind you.

JUDY. I know, but....

*(***MAURICE*** comes to them.)*

MAURICE. Please – I ask you one more time – let us try to find you a nice hotel. We pay the difference.

FRED. Sorry – we're not going to any hotel. It's a villa holiday we booked, and we're staying.

MAURICE. Then it seems there is only one thing to do.

FRED. What's that?

MAURICE. We have to share.

JUDY. Share?

FRED. Share?

MAURICE. We share the house. It's big. We can be separated. We can be private. We stay here together.

JUDY. But you don't understand. We're not the only....

FRED. *(stopping her)* Shush! *(to MAURICE)* How long you here for?

MAURICE. Two weeks, like you.

FRED. You mean we spend the whole holiday here together?

MAURICE. What else can we do? Either we fight a duel with the pistols, or we have to share.

FRED. Well, I dunno....

JUDY. Could be quite fun, Fred.

FRED. What about cooking and everything?

MAURICE. *(shrugging)* Some nights you go to a restaurant, some nights we go. We take in turn.

FRED. What about the rent?

MAURICE. You pay half.

JUDY. That'd be fair.

FRED. I dunno.

MAURICE. Have you another idea?

FRED. Well...bit of a funny arrangement.

MAURICE. It's called the Common Market. I know you British don't like it, but maybe you can try.

FRED. What if we don't get on?

MAURICE. You are always free to leave.

FRED. Yeh, thanks.

JUDY. I think it's the best way, Fred.

MAURICE. It is the *only* way.

FRED. Well, all right, but...

JUDY. But Fred – you'll have to say to them...I mean, what about...? *(nods towards the second bedrooms)*

FRED. Yeh. Look, there's something we should, er....

MAURICE. I know, the bedrooms. This is easy. We take the first bedroom here. You have all the other rooms over there. You have two bedrooms, you have your own bathroom, you have...

FRED. Oh no, no, no...

MAURICE. What?

FRED. That bedroom's ours. We've already moved in.

YVETTE. *(jumping in)* Ah, non! Zis bedroom is ours!

JUDY. No – it's ours. Our cases are in there.

YVETTE. Non! Absolument non!

MAURICE. No, you see it's our own personal bedroom, this. We have our clothes in the cupboard, we have all our things in the bathroom....

JUDY. Oh, Fred!

FRED. Well I'm sorry about that, but we've already picked that room. My wife's set her heart on it, you see. I'm afraid that's part of the deal.

YVETTE. Non! I must have my bedroom. It's not fair!

MAURICE. Please. For the sake of the entente cordiale.

FRED. Listen, chum – you can stick the entente cordiale up your vive la France! We've given in on the bloody house – we at least get to choose bedrooms.

JUDY. Oh, but Fred, if they're in one of those bedrooms, what about, you know...?

FRED. What about you know if *we're* in one of those bedrooms? They'll all have to pig in together, won't they, and see how the entente cordiale works then.

MAURICE. Pig in? What is this?

FRED. Never mind. The point is, it's not negotiable. We have that room, or the deal's off. We'll let you choose when to use the kitchen first – how's that?

YVETTE. Non! Maurice!

MAURICE. *(hopelessly)* Qu'est ce que je peux faire?

YVETTE. *(losing her cool)* You are terrible, you English! You are selfish, you are bad! You have no morals. I despise you!

FRED. Oh well, that's a good start. I can see this is going to be a very friendly holiday.

YVETTE. Maurice! *(She bursts into tears on MAURICE's shoulder.)*

JUDY. Oh gawd, Fred. Now look what you've done.

FRED. It wasn't my fault. It wasn't me started hurling abuse.

JUDY. Well, we have sort of pinched their home, haven't we?

FRED. You wanted that room!

JUDY. Well, I know, but…

FRED. Are you going to take their side now? Whose fault is it this all happened in the first place?

JUDY. Well, I can understand how she feels. We could perhaps give them their bedroom…

FRED. No! That's not negotiable. I'm not listening to you-know-who at it all night long on the other side of the wall.

JUDY. *(indicating the others)* Well they'll have to, won't they?

FRED. They're used to it – they're French.

JUDY. Fred!

FRED. They'll be at it the same time themselves. They can all heave ho together.

MAURICE. What is this?

FRED. Never mind.

JUDY. *(whispering in his ear)* You'll have to tell them.

FRED. I will, I will. Let's all calm down first.

MAURICE. O.K. We make a deal. You have the bedroom first week – we have it second.

YVETTE. Oh, Maurice…

MAURICE. Shh.

JUDY. That's fair, Fred.

FRED. *(grudging)* Well, all right. We dunno who'll be in whose bedroom by then anyway – ha, ha?

JUDY. Fred!

FRED. Only joking.

YVETTE. This is affreux! The holiday is spoiled.

JUDY. *(consoling)* Don't worry, love. It'll work out. It'll be quite fun once we've all settled in.

YVETTE. Your husband is a pig!

FRED. Thanks.

JUDY. He's quite nice really – once you get to know him.

YVETTE. Thank you, I don't wish to know him. I don't wish to be near him!

FRED. Pity. Wouldn't mind being near myself.

JUDY. Fred! What's the matter with you?

FRED. Well I've got as much chance with her as with you, haven't I?

JUDY. *(hissing)* Bloody hell, Fred! Just because I won't strip off the moment we get in the door! Good job I didn't, isn't it? They'd have walked right in on us.

FRED. Yeh, well that would've started things off with a bang, wouldn't it – ha, ha? Might have been a lot more fun that way.

JUDY. You're impossible sometimes. *(turns to the others)* Perhaps we'd better introduce ourselves. I'm Judy, and he's Fred.

MAURICE. *(resigned)* Maurice and Yvette.

JUDY. How d'you do. *(shakes hands with him)* I'm ever so sorry about it all. It's just bad luck.

MAURICE. Yes.

JUDY. It's a lovely place you've got here though. Did you do it all up yourselves?

MAURICE. My wife did it, yes.

JUDY. Lovely. *(to* YVETTE*)* You've got very good taste.

YVETTE. *(grudging)* Thank you.

MAURICE. *(gesturing to the guest wing)* We design it so friends can come, and two couples are private together. At least that is one good thing.

JUDY. Oh, yes…*(looks at* FRED*)* Er…yes well, there is something else actually.

MAURICE. What?

JUDY. There's something we haven't told you. Fred?

FRED. What?

JUDY. Come on, Fred. You'll have to tell them.

MAURICE. What?

YVETTE. What?

FRED. Yes, well…um…it's a bit awkward actually.

MAURICE. What?

YVETTE. What?

FRED. The thing is, you see…. *(pause)*

MAURICE. *What?*

FRED. We've got some other friends coming.

(pause)

MAURICE. What?

YVETTE. What?

FRED. Yeh. They're sharing the house with us.

MAURICE. Sharing the house?

FRED. Yeh. Well it's a bit big for just two, isn't it – ha, ha?

YVETTE. They're coming here?

JUDY. Yes.

MAURICE. When?

FRED. *(looking at his watch)* Any moment actually. They're a bit late.

YVETTE. *(screaming)* Ahhhh!

MAURICE. *(going to her)* Yvette, non!

(She smacks him hard round the face. He staggers back.)

YVETTE. C'est de ta faut, tout ca!

JUDY. Oh, listen, love…

FRED. *(going to* YVETTE*)* Look I'm sorry, but they're very nice. You'll love them…

(She smacks him too.)

Oof!

YVETTE. I will not love them! I will hate them! I hate you too! *(to* MAURICE*)* I hate *you!* I hate everybody!

JUDY. Oh God, Fred – do something.

FRED. What? What can I do? She's insane!

JUDY. Christ! I wish we'd gone to Torquay.

YVETTE. Maurice, c'est impossible! Je retourne a Paris.

MAURICE. Non, chérie….

YVETTE. Je n'reste pas ici avec ces…ces….

FRED. Careful now. Remember the entente cordiale.

YVETTE. Ils sont affreux!

FRED. I bet that was rude.

MAURICE. Chérie, we must do the best. We can still have a nice time.

YVETTE. How? How a nice time with people like this?

JUDY. We're not so bad, love. Not when you get to know us.

YVETTE. I told you, I don't wish to know you! I don't wish to see you, or hear you, or…or smell you!

FRED. Charming!

JUDY. O.K. but you can't go back to Paris. Not now. It's all arranged.

YVETTE. *(shaking with frustration)* Urrr!

MAURICE. Chérie – s'il te plait. *(to* FRED*)* Where are these friends? How they come?

FRED. They're flying to Nice, taking a taxi from there. We took the Channel Tunnel and drove down, you see.

MAURICE. Ah.

JUDY. We go on holiday every year together, you see.

FRED. They should be here by now. We planned to arrive together.

MAURICE. This is not a good arrangement. We are not happy.

FRED. No. Us neither.

YVETTE. You understand – we keep totalement apart. We don't speak together, we don't eat together, we don't go in the piscine together. Nothing!

FRED. Fair enough.

YVETTE. *(to MAURICE)* The very first bad thing, I go back to Paris!

MAURICE. Oui, chérie.

YVETTE. C'est tout!

JUDY. Fred.

FRED. What?

JUDY. We must give them their room.

FRED. What?

JUDY. It's only fair.

FRED. No.

JUDY. *(determined)* Yes, Fred. We can't put them next door to Shaun and Moira. We can't have them sharing bathrooms. Can you imagine it?

FRED. Can you imagine *us* sharing? It'll be like a farmyard in there!

JUDY. Well that's why we can't put them there. It's their house, it's not fair.

FRED. Bloody hell! This is becoming a nightmare!

JUDY. *(to the others)* You have the main bedroom. We'll move our stuff out.

MAURICE. Thank you, madame. That's very kind of you. Say thank you, Yvette.

YVETTE. *(sulking)* Non.

MAURICE. Ah! *(to JUDY)* Pardon.

JUDY. Don't worry. I know how she feels.

FRED. You'd better move in with them too – you'll all get on fine.

JUDY. Fred!

FRED. Well…

JUDY. Look, we've got to make the most of this situation. We're stuck with it.

FRED. Gawd knows what Shaun is going to say when he walks in. Let alone Moira.

JUDY. Oh, Moira'll quite enjoy it. Especially when she meets Gerard Dépardieu here.

FRED. You what?

JUDY. You know what a flirt she is.

FRED. Yes, I do.

MAURICE. Flirt? What is this?

JUDY. Oh, you'll see. You'll like Moira.

MAURICE. Ah.

JUDY. They're great fun, our friends. They're Irish.

YVETTE. Irelandais?

JUDY. Yes.

YVETTE. Mon dieu!

JUDY. Don't you like the Irish?

MAURICE. They can be very charming.

YVETTE. Ils sont impossible.

JUDY. Impossible, yes. But they're lovely too. Aren't they, Fred?

FRED. Lovely.

MAURICE. It's going to be quite a er…bouillabaisse, isn't it?

FRED. A what?

MAURICE. How you say – stew?

FRED. You could say that – yeh. European stew. Garlic and blarney all mixed together.

JUDY. Well at least that's more interesting than just Irish stew and Lancashire hotpot. A touch of French cuisine might spice it up a bit.

FRED. Oh, getting quite keen now, are you? Getting all enthusiastic now?

JUDY. Well, it's a chance to make friends, isn't it? I must say, Maurice, I do like your French cooking.

MAURICE. Thank you, madame. There are some very good restaurants around.

JUDY. Oh, you must tell us where to go.

YVETTE. Attention, Maurice. Pas celui que l'on préfère!

MAURICE. *(dismissive)* Ohh…Pourquoi pas?

YVETTE. Non. Il est pour nous.

JUDY. Don't worry, love. We won't intrude.

MAURICE. Maybe the last night – if we are all still friends, ha, ha – we all go together.

JUDY. That would be nice. Wouldn't it, Fred?

FRED. Lovely.

JUDY. Well now, that's all settled. Fred – bring our suitcases. We'll go and unpack through there.

(FRED doesn't move.)

Now, Fred!

(He reluctantly goes to get the cases.)

I'm sure we'll all have a lovely time.

MAURICE. I hope so, madame.

JUDY. Judy, please.

MAURICE. *(nodding)* Judy.

JUDY. *(nodding after FRED)* You can call him what you like. He gets called everything under the sun.

(She goes off towards the other bedrooms. **MAURICE** *turns to* **YVETTE** *and gestures hopelessly.)*

YVETTE. Je te déteste.

MAURICE. C'est pas d'ma faute.

YVETTE. Oui, c'est d'ta faute.

MAURICE. Non.

YVETTE. Oui! Je te déteste!

(FRED staggers out of the bedroom with the suitcases. Smiles awkwardly.)

FRED. Sorry.

(heaves them across to the other side)

MAURICE. You bring enough clothes, eh?

FRED. They're mostly hers. Why do women always have to pack for a year, eh?

MAURICE. Ah, yes. My wife is the same.

YVETTE. Maurice!

MAURICE. C'est vrais. *(to* FRED*)* She has clothes in there enough to start a shop, and all she wears is a bikini.

FRED. I look forward to seeing that.

YVETTE. What?

FRED. Nothing. I never said a thing.

(hurries off with the cases)

YVETTE. Ah, mon dieu!

MAURICE. It is a compliment.

YVETTE. I don't wish compliments from him.

MAURICE. It's the first time you complain.

YVETTE. What you mean?

MAURICE. Rien. Ne te fâche pas, Yvette. We have to make the best.

YVETTE. O.K. but I'm not happy.

MAURICE. It's your problem – you're never happy.

YVETTE. You want I punch your nose?

(He shrugs and goes to pick up their stuff.)

MAURICE. Viens.

YVETTE. Tu l'fais.

(He takes the stuff through to the bedroom. She comes and gazes out front at the view.)

YVETTE. *(to herself)* Chez moi. Hah!

(FRED returns. Sees her. Comes diffidently down-stage.)

FRED. I've left her unpacking. She'll be a while. Like half a day.

YVETTE. *(curt)* Ah.

(pause)

FRED. I'm sorry we've spoilt your holiday.

YVETTE. *(shrugging)* Eh.

FRED. I can imagine how you were looking forward to it. Peace and quiet...

YVETTE. C'est la vie.

FRED. C'est la vie. Yes, I can understand quite a lot of French, you know. Funny that. I never learnt it.

YVETTE. We give many expressions to the world.

FRED. Yeh. Bon appetit...au revoir...toujours l'amour. That's all you need to get along really, isn't it?

YVETTE. Toujours l'amour? The English believe that?

FRED. Yeh – why not?

YVETTE. You are not so romantic.

FRED. Oh, don't you believe it, love. The English are as romantic as anybody. They just don't talk about it so much.

YVETTE. You? You are romantic?

FRED. Oh, yeh. Not half.

YVETTE. You don't look so.

FRED. Yeh, well...I've kind of lost the touch.

YVETTE. I'm sorry I hit you.

FRED. S'all right. I haven't been slapped by a woman for a long time. Quite exciting really.

YVETTE. Ha. I slap Maurice all the time. He doesn't find it exciting.

FRED. Does he smack you back?

YVETTE. He doesn't dare. Would you?

FRED. Oh yeh. And probably not on the cheek – ha, ha. *(a beat)* See, I told you we were romantic.

(She digests that. There is the sound of a car outside.)

Ah. Sounds like them.

YVETTE. Ah mon dieu.

FRED. Don't worry – you'll like them. The Irish are *very* romantic.

(MAURICE *returns.*)

MAURICE. It's your friends?

FRED. *(going to the door)* I think so.

(JUDY *returns.*)

JUDY. Is it them?

FRED. *(peering through the upstage window)* I think so. It's a taxi. *(returns)* Look, er…I think it might be better if we explain the situation before they meet you – know what I mean? It's a bit awkward.

MAURICE. Ah, yes. Yvette – we go in the bedroom.

YVETTE. When they know, perhaps they go away again.

FRED. I wouldn't count on it.

(MAURICE *and* YVETTE *go off to the main bedroom.*)

JUDY. Oh lord, Fred, I wonder how they'll take it.

FRED. Probably a lot better than the Frenchies. Shaun doesn't mind who's around, as long as they laugh at his jokes.

JUDY. Well, open the door.

(He goes to the door as the sound of a car drawing away is heard from outside. He stops at the sound of angry voices.)

MOIRA. *(off)* That was embarrassing, Shaun. That was really embarrassing!

SHAUN. *(off)* For God's sake, woman – he didn't deserve a tip!

MOIRA. You always tip in France!

SHAUN. Not when they've ripped us off a bloody fortune to get here, and driven us half round Provence into the bargain, you don't!

MOIRA. It wasn't his fault it was hard to find.

SHAUN. He's a taxi driver, isn't he? He should bloody know where to go!

(FRED *opens the door.*)

FRED. Voila, mes amis!

(SHAUN *and* MOIRA *enter with suitcases. They both have gentle Irish lilts.*)

SHAUN. Aha! So you beat us to it.

MOIRA. Oh lord, Fred! Have we had a time getting here!

SHAUN. Delayed flight naturally.

MOIRA. Couldn't find a taxi driver who'd bring us here.

SHAUN. And when we finally did, he charged us a ruddy arm and a leg! The French are all crooks if you ask me.

FRED. Shh! Never mind – you've made it now. Give us your case, Moira.

JUDY. *(kissing them)* Hello, Fred, hello, Moira – welcome chez nous!

SHAUN. Hello, love. *(looking round)* Hey, this is nice!

MOIRA. This is beautiful! Better than last year, eh, Fred?

FRED. Don't talk about last year. Horrormolinos, that was.

JUDY. This is real class.

SHAUN. *(looking out front)* Would you look at that view!

(*They all come down-stage.*)

JUDY. The pool's down there.

MOIRA. Oh, look at the pool, Shaun! Can't wait to get in there.

SHAUN. Yes, sure. Tops off, tits out, and in the water, eh girls?

MOIRA. Now, Shaun – don't start all that the moment we get here.

SHAUN. Well, for God's sake, that's what France is all about, isn't it? *(husky)* Je t'aime...mon amour...

MOIRA. Oh, Shaun!

FRED. Same old Shaun.

JUDY. Yes. Well, er...we can't all go wild just yet. I'm afraid there's.... there's been a bit of a hitch.

SHAUN. Hitch?

JUDY. Tell them, Fred.

FRED. Ych, er...the thing is, the agents have sort of cocked up.

MOIRA. What d'you mean?

FRED. Well, they didn't tell the owners of the house that they'd let it at the last minute.

JUDY. And the owners didn't tell the agents they wanted to use it themselves.

SHAUN. So what are you saying?

FRED. They're here too.

SHAUN. Who are?

JUDY. The owners.

MOIRA. The owners?

FRED. They're French. From Paris.

JUDY. They're in the bedroom.

SHAUN. Let me get this right. We're sharing the house with the froggy owners?

FRED. Shhh! They're just in there.

MOIRA. There's going to be six of us here?

JUDY. Yes. They're very nice. You'll like him, Moira. He's a dishy Frenchman.

FRED. And she's a bit of all right too – if you keep clear of her temper.

SHAUN. Temper?

JUDY. Well they weren't very happy when they found us here, and she threw a bit of a wobbly.

FRED. That's an understatement. She nearly knocked her husband's head off – followed by mine.

JUDY. We all had a bit of a show-down. They were demanding we left, and Fred was demanding they left, and she was threatening to go back to Paris on her own, and.... well I'm glad you weren't here, that's all.

SHAUN. Bloody hell! Bang goes our nice private holiday.

FRED. We had to give in in the end, and agree to share. We're only paying half price. It means a bit more for the old table d'hote.

MOIRA. Do we have to speak French to them?

JUDY. Don't worry – they speak good English.

FRED. With the odd pardon-my-French thrown in.

SHAUN. So what are they doing in there?

FRED. Waiting for us to explain it to you. We thought it best they weren't here in case you went doolally.

SHAUN. I might have done just that. Jesus Christ!

MOIRA. Oh well, Shaun, I suppose we'll have to make the best of it. But don't embarrass us, please.

SHAUN. Me, embarrassing – never!

JUDY. We've agreed to keep separate anyway. We're cooking separately, and we've let them have the master bedroom through there. We're all over there in that half.

SHAUN. Oh, right. That's the red light district then, is it?

MOIRA. Now, Shaun...

SHAUN. Well, I hope the French presence isn't going to mean we have to cut down on standard procedures, does it?

MOIRA. *(embarrassed)* For heaven's sake, Shaun!

FRED. Oh gawd. I hope you two aren't going to keep us awake half the night.

SHAUN. Of course not. We're the height of discretion.

FRED. Yes, I've heard your discretion. So can all the neighbours.

SHAUN. Well the Irish can't help being a lusty nation.

MOIRA. *(long-suffering)* Mother of God...

SHAUN. Sure, the French are supposed to be the same, aren't they? That's what we're always told.

FRED. I dunno, but we'd better get them in here. It's time you met them.

(goes to the main bedroom door and knocks)

Hello. Madame et monsieur. Are you there?

(The door opens and **MAURICE** *and* **YVETTE** *come out.)*

These are our friends from Ireland. Shaun and Moira. This is, er...

MAURICE. I am Maurice. My wife Yvette. How do you do.

SHAUN. Ah, pleased to meet you.

MOIRA. Me too. How d'you do.

(They all shake hands.)

SHAUN. We've heard about the mix up.

MAURICE. I am sorry. The fault of the agent...

YVETTE. And my husband.

JUDY. Never mind whose fault it was. We're all going to have a great time together. *(to the French)* We've explained the arrangement.

MOIRA. I'm sure we'll all get along fine.

SHAUN. Absolutely!

MAURICE. I am sure.

FRED. As Maurice here says, it's a test of the European union, isn't it?

SHAUN. Ah, that's a good point.

MOIRA. That's right.

SHAUN. *(declaims)* All nations shall come together...as long as the bed springs hold out.

JUDY. Shaun!

(together)

MOIRA. Shaun!

FRED. Same old Shaun.

MAURICE. *(puzzled)* Pardon?

YVETTE. I'm sorry, I don't understand this. Can you explain, please?

(The others all stand back and look at SHAUN. He looks abashed.)

SHAUN. Er, well....

(blackout)

Scene Two

(An hour or so later. SHAUN *sits alone on the patio couch reading an Irish newspaper as he swings idly. He is dressed the same, except for having taken off his jacket and donned a concessionary straw hat.)*

*(*JUDY *comes onto the terrace from the swimming pool. She is wearing a swimsuit with a flimsy beach wrap around the waist.)*

JUDY. Shaun! Where've you been? We were waiting for you.

SHAUN. Ah, you know me. Have to take the sun in stages.

JUDY. Where are the Frenchies?

SHAUN. Gone off to the village shop. They said we can shop tonight when we go out to eat. It stays open late.

JUDY. Right.

SHAUN. You look good in that outfit.

JUDY. I can't say the same about you. You might at least get your shoes and socks off.

SHAUN. Yes – well….

(He gets up from the couch. They look at each other for a moment, and then go into a passionate embrace.)

JUDY. *(in between kisses)* Oh, Shaun…I've missed you. It's been ages.

SHAUN. *(throwing his sun hat down)* Oh, too long, too long.

JUDY. Why can't you come over to London more often?

SHAUN. I can't. The business won't take it. And Moira's suspicious as it is.

JUDY. Oh, Shaun…God I want you!

SHAUN. Are the others safe by the pool?

JUDY. I think so. Where can we go?

SHAUN. Not the bedrooms. They could walk in on us. Oh God, I can't wait.

JUDY. Me neither.

SHAUN. Come inside. We'll hear if anyone comes.

(He leads her into the house and behind the sofa. They embrace passionately, and disappear down behind the sofa whence only their voices are heard.)

JUDY. Not on the tiles, Shaun.

SHAUN. What?

JUDY. I'll bruise me bum.

SHAUN. Hang on….

(SHAUN's arm appears over the sofa, gropes around, finds a cushion and disappears with it.)

Put this under you.

JUDY. Oh Shaun….

SHAUN. Oh God, Judy, Judy….

(A few moments pass, punctuated by scuffling and the odd judder from the sofa. Then FRED calls off-stage.)

FRED. Judy?

(Instant silence from behind the sofa. FRED appears on the terrace, dressed in floppy swim shorts and open shirt.)

FRED. Judy!

(SHAUN's head appears briefly above the back of the sofa. He sees FRED.)

SHAUN. Jesus!

(Bobs back down again. FRED enters.)

FRED. Judy?

(Goes off to the bedrooms, passing the sofa on his way but noticing nothing. Disappears. SHAUN crawls out from behind the sofa towards the terrace, his trousers half over his hips. Frantically scrambles onto the patio couch and rearranges himself. JUDY scurries out from behind the sofa, pulling up her straps. Scrabbles to the kitchen area, and disappears behind the breakfast bar, whence come cupboard and crockery sounds. MOIRA comes along the terrace wearing a beach robe.)

MOIRA. There you are, Shaun. Still in your trousers? What are you doing here?

SHAUN. *(hiding his disarranged flies with the newspaper)* Er… good question. I'm just sliding into things gently, darlin'. Know what I mean?

MOIRA. It's too nice to waste time reading papers. It's gorgeous down by the pool.

SHAUN. Yes, yes, I'm sure. I'll, er…

(FRED returns from the bedrooms.)

FRED. Judy? Judy?

(JUDY's head appears over the breakfast bar.)

JUDY. *(innocently)* Hello, darling.

FRED. There you are! Where the hell d'you get to?

JUDY. I was just, er…just checking out the kitchen. Seeing what they've got.

FRED. I just came through here.

JUDY. Did you, love?

FRED. Didn't you hear me calling?

JUDY. Oh, I know. *(indicates the main bedroom)* I sneaked in there to have another look at their lovely bathroom. I must have been there.

(MOIRA comes upstage from the terrace.)

FRED. I wish to God you'd forget about kitchens and bathrooms for once in your life. *(to MOIRA)* Obsessed she is! You're not like that, are you, Moira?

MOIRA. Well, they are important to a woman, Fred.

FRED. I know, but she'll spend the whole holiday cleaning cupboards if she gets her way.

JUDY. Oh, come on, Fred. I was just looking.

FRED. *(seeing SHAUN on the terrace)* And Shaun – there you are! Bloody hell – where's everyone been hiding?

SHAUN. *(jerking a thumb over his shoulder)* I, er…went for a scout round the other side.

FRED. Oh, yeh. Up to no good in the bushes already?

SHAUN. *(nodding)* That would have been sensible.

FRED. What?

SHAUN. Nothing. There's not much round there.

FRED. *(looking at his watch)* Well, look now – time's getting on. Where are the Frenchies?

JUDY. Gone shopping.

FRED. Well, it must be nearly cocktail hour. How are we going to play this?

SHAUN. *(getting up from the couch)* Well, where do they keep the booze?

MOIRA. Shaun, we can't drink theirs!

FRED. No, we ought to clear out and leave the place free for them.

SHAUN. All right, let's go off to the village, and suss out the local drinking holes.

MOIRA. We've got to shop for breakfast as well.

JUDY. Yes, I need some more shampoo and stuff.

FRED. Oh gawd – here we go. She'll be buying up half the village before we've started.

JUDY. Fred!

FRED. Right, you girls go and get changed – and don't take all night about it – and Shaun and me'll get our after-shave on, and we'll leave in twenty minutes. How's that?

JUDY. Oh, give us a bit longer, Fred.

FRED. For god's sake, how long do you want? Change your knickers, squirt of perfume – s'all you need here!

JUDY. We have to wash our hair. We've been in the pool.

FRED. It's clean water, isn't it? What's the point of washing off clean water with more clean water?

MOIRA. It is full of chlorine and stuff, Fred.

FRED. Chlorine's good for hair – sterilises it. Gawd, I'll never understand it, eh Shaun? – the less they have to put on, the longer it takes.

SHAUN. Ah, well...let them do their thing, Fred.

FRED. I do want to eat before midnight. Go on then, girls. Chop, chop.

(The women go off. SHAUN searches for drink.)

FRED. *(cont.)* If she stopped washing her hair she'd solve the global warming problem overnight. Drives me crackers sometimes, Shaun.

SHAUN. What's that?

FRED. Judy and her bloody nonsense. *(mimics)* 'Got to have the right pan for this, got to have the right lotion for that.' Polish the potatoes, hoover the doormat – bloody hell, it's a nightmare! She spends all day fiddling about with petty little stuff like that, and never has any time left for real living. Know what I mean?

SHAUN. Ah, well...*(finds some wine)* Aha! Here we are. Drink?

FRED. Oh yeh – why not? She never seems to have a thought for the things that really matter, like she used to. Remember the first year we all met – in Majorca?

SHAUN. Yeh.

FRED. Wonderful holiday that, wasn't it? All of us full of passion and plans. Dreaming all day and humping all night. Best holiday we've ever had that.

SHAUN. Yeh.

FRED. Never been as good since. The dreams have all gone, and she'll hardly even drop her knickers any more in case it puts a crease in them. Moira's not like that, is she?

SHAUN. Well, they all get a bit like that. It's what happens when domesticity creeps in.

FRED. Creeps in? It's more like a full-scale invasion in our house.

SHAUN. Well, sometimes, you know Fred, it's compensation for...

FRED. For what?

SHAUN. I dunno...a lack of excitement in their lives.

FRED. Excitement? I've brought her to the bloody Riviera – what more excitement can you want?

SHAUN. Yes, but not just at holiday time. You know...

FRED. Well, I can't be giving her thrills all day long, can I? I've got a business to run. We've had kids to bring up.

SHAUN. Sure. Well it's a common problem.

FRED. I mean, this is the first time you and us have been able to take a holiday without all the kids along, isn't it? I really thought it was a chance to get back to, you know...a bit of real romance.

SHAUN. Real sex, you mean.

FRED. Not just sex, but...well yeh, a bit of that would be nice too. But you know what I'm saying, Shaun?

SHAUN. Tell me, Fred...

FRED. What?

SHAUN. You haven't, er...ever been tempted to...you know, look for your excitement elsewhere, have you?

FRED. Me? I should be so lucky.

SHAUN. You wouldn't say no then?

FRED. I never get the chance. Up to my eyes all day...and doing her bloody chores around the house all my spare time. The odd weekend we get away, we usually have to take her bloody mother with us!

SHAUN. Yes.

FRED. What about you? You and Moira seem all right...

SHAUN. Ah, well...

FRED. But do you ever get the urge to cut loose?

SHAUN. Well...it's a nice idea sometimes, isn't it?

FRED. At least you get away on the business from time to time.

SHAUN. Occasionally.

FRED. You must be tempted to have a bit of totty available somewhere.

SHAUN. Ah, well...I'm a Catholic, Fred.

FRED. What's that got to do with anything?

SHAUN. Not a lot, that's true.

FRED. Well I'll tell you something. This time I'm going to eat and drink myself silly, I'm going to soak in this beautiful place, and I'm going to roger something, even if it's that's bloody statue down by the pool!

SHAUN. I wish I could help. I'd offer to swap partners for a bit, but I don't think it'd go down too well.

FRED. Oh yeh – ha, ha. Imagine how the girls would react to that! Do our friendship no end of good, that would.

SHAUN. Let's change the subject. It's getting me all worked up.

FRED. Anything gets you worked up.

(A car is heard pulling up outside.)

SHAUN. Ah, sounds like the Frenchies back.

FRED. Yeh. Now that little Yvette – cor, she's a scorcher, eh?

SHAUN. I wouldn't go messing with that, Fred. I wouldn't want him coming after me with a carving knife in one hand and a garlic crusher in the other.

FRED. Oh, no way. Not me.

(The front door opens, and **MAURICE** *and* **YVETTE** *enter carrying several large bags of groceries.)*

YVETTE. Poof!

MAURICE. Ah! That's heavy.

FRED. Here, let me help. *(helps them to the kitchen)* Blimey – you eat well, you French.

MAURICE. Well, we bring some dinner for all of us. We thought it would be good to make friends...start again...get to know each other.

SHAUN. Oh, that's nice.

FRED. Oh, but look – you wanted your privacy. Yvette was...

MAURICE. Oh no, she wants it too. She's sorry she loses her temper.

YVETTE. Yes – please. We all have dinner tonight, and then tomorrow we can be separate.

MAURICE. Voila!

FRED. Well, that's kind of you. What d'you say, Shaun?

SHAUN. Yes, that'd be lovely. Very friendly. I'll, er...I'll go and tell the girls, shall I? *(goes off)*

FRED. *(to the others)* I'll give you a hand. What else do you need? What about drinks and stuff? Can we....?

MAURICE. No, no – we have plenty here in the cave, er... cellar. I keep it locked, but we have wine, champagne, everything.

FRED. It doesn't seem right really, after...

MAURICE. No, no. We want to make friends. It will be nice.

YVETTE. Yes. I bring the rest from the car.

MAURICE. Let me help.

YVETTE. Non, non...

(She goes off. **MAURICE** *busies himself in the kitchen area.* **FRED** *hovers.)*

FRED. Got a great set-up here, Maurice.

MAURICE. Set up?

FRED. Good life. Home in Paris, house down here. Very nice.

MAURICE. Ah, yes. But life is not always so easy, you know.

FRED. No?

MAURICE. I have much stress in Paris. Work hard. Not easy always to come away when we wish.

FRED. Oh, yeh. I know what it's like.

(Comes down-stage and sits in the sofa looking out of the terrace doors.)

Still – when you do get down, and you can sit here looking at that view, you must think, well there are compensations.

MAURICE. Oh, yes.

FRED. You got kids?

MAURICE. Er...no. Yvette, she cannot have children.

FRED. Oh, that's a pity.

MAURICE. *(shrugging)* C'est la vie. But sometimes she is unhappy.

FRED. Yeh, well – kids can be a trial sometimes too, you know.

MAURICE. You like champagne? You and your friends?

FRED. You bet. Not half!

MAURICE. Good. I'll, er....

(He goes off-stage from the kitchen area, but FRED *does not notice he has gone, and continues talking.)*

FRED. Yeh – kids! You love 'em, but the little buggers can take over your life as well, know what I mean? Sometimes doesn't leave you with much.

*(*YVETTE *returns with more bags.* FRED *doesn't notice – thinks the sounds are still* MAURICE*)*

Now you may not have kids, but you've got a cracking wife. Sexy and intelligent. Still got some spark in her. That's worth a lot, believe me.

*(*YVETTE *listens from the kitchen area.)*

I tell you, I'd rather have a wife that loses her cool sometimes in the kitchen, as long as she gets hot as well in the bedroom. *(over his shoulder)* Know what I mean?

YVETTE. Yes, I know what you mean.

FRED. Oh bloody hell!

(leaps up and stares at her)

Sorry, I...didn't realise – I....

YVETTE. It's all right. Don't be embarrassed.

FRED. Well, I mean, I....

YVETTE. I understand what you are saying.

FRED. Do you? Sorry, it was man's talk. Not very tactful...

YVETTE. I have – what you say...a wide mind?

FRED. Broad mind. That's good.

YVETTE. So – your wife, she...

FRED. What?

YVETTE. Does not get, er...hot in the bedroom?

FRED. *(embarrassed)* Oh, well...I didn't mean.... well she used to all right. But when you've been married a long time, it's just...you can all get a bit bored with it, can't you?

YVETTE. Yes, you can.

(pause)

FRED. You too?

YVETTE. Of course. It's natural.

FRED. Yeh – right.

YVETTE. We have a rude saying in France.

FRED. What's that?

YVETTE. The English husband reads sexy magazines, the Italian husband watches sexy films, the German goes to sexy clubs, and the Frenchman keeps a mistress.

FRED. Oh yeh – ha, ha. That's good. Is it true?

YVETTE. *(shrugging)* You tell me.

FRED. I mean, has your husband got a mistress?

YVETTE. Maybe. I don't ask.

FRED. Sensible.

YVETTE. You?

FRED. I should be so lucky. I don't even get to see sexy magazines.

YVETTE. Ah. Poor Fred.

*(**MAURICE** returns with bottles of wine and champagne.)*

MAURICE. Voila!

FRED. Oh, terrific!

MAURICE. *(putting down the bottles)* Why poor Fred?

FRED. Er…

YVETTE. He doesn't have a mistress.

MAURICE. Ah. Poor Fred.

YVETTE. He wants to know if you have a mistress.

MAURICE. Me? I don't dare. *(waves a bottle)* Yvette would murder me.

YVETTE. *(to **FRED**)* Voila.

MAURICE. But a man can dream, eh Fred?

FRED. Yeh.

YVETTE. Dreams I allow.

(**MOIRA** *comes in from the bedrooms.*)

MOIRA. Oh. What's all this? What's going on here?

FRED. Didn't Shaun tell you?

MOIRA. Tell me what?

FRED. Maurice and Yvette have invited us to dinner tonight.

MOIRA. Oh, that's nice.

FRED. Didn't he say?

MOIRA. Shaun? I haven't seen him. Where is he?

FRED. He went off to find you.

MOIRA. Ah – I must have been in the bathroom. Well, that's really nice.

MAURICE. We want we should all be friends. I make a special dinner for us.

MOIRA. (*oozing up to the breakfast bar*) Oo, you mean you cook as well, Maurice.

MAURICE. As well as what?

MOIRA. As well as keep fit and brown, and speak with a charming accent, and do all those other lovely French things.

FRED. Now, Moira, down girl.

MOIRA. I'm just being friendly back, Fred.

FRED. Yeh, we all know what your friendly means. Watch yourself, Maurice – she'll have your trousers off before you can say Eiffel Tower.

MOIRA. Don't be ridiculous, Fred! (*to* **MAURICE**) I'm not like that at all, Maurice. I just have a warm heart and a friendly Irish way with me.

MAURICE. That's very nice. I like that.

YVETTE. (*tart*) Oh yes, he likes that very much.

FRED. Yes, well this is all rife with innuendo and possibilities, isn't it? Where the bloody hell have the others got to?

MOIRA. I don't know.

FRED. (*calling*) Judy!

MOIRA. So what are you going to cook for us, Maurice?

MAURICE. Ah, this is surprise.

MOIRA. Oh goody, I love surprises.

MAURICE. The good chef, he never says what he's going to cook – then if it doesn't go well, he can say it's something else.

MOIRA. Yes, I understand that. My cooking always turns out to be something else. *(turns to* YVETTE*)* So, do you take it in turns to cook in your household, Yvette?

YVETTE. We share, yes. But Maurice is a better cook than me.

MOIRA. Goodness! Now there's something, eh Fred?

FRED. Yeh.

MAURICE. Well…I am a better everything than her.

YVETTE. *(hands on hips)* Oh.

MOIRA. Oo!

MAURICE. I am a man. The man is always better at doing things. Eh, Fred?

FRED. Blimey, Maurice.

MAURICE. The woman – she is better at feeling things.

YVETTE. Hah!

FRED. Judy'd have my goolies if I said something like that!

MAURICE. Goolies?

FRED. You can guess.

MAURICE. But it's true, no?

MOIRA. Well now, Maurice, I'd heard that French men were chauvinists, but I didn't really believe it.

MAURICE. Not so, just realists.

FRED. Are you going to stand there and let him get away with that, Yvette?

YVETTE. *(dismissive)* Ah! I stop arguing with him a long time ago.

MAURICE. You see? The man even argues better – because we have the logic.

YVETTE. The logic and the bullshit.

MAURICE. I think we will have a very interesting discussion with the dinner tonight, eh Fred?

FRED. Bloody hell, if it's all going to be like that, Maurice, the dinner might end on the ceiling.

MAURICE. Oh, I just make a provocation so we can have a good argument. The British don't like to contest with words, eh?

FRED. Oh, yes. We just don't like to end in a contest with knives. Where are those two? *(calls)* Judy! Shaun!

MAURICE. *(popping a champagne cork)* We have a drink now to – what you say? – start rolling the ball.

(JUDY comes in looking somewhat dishevelled.)

JUDY. *(straightening her hair)* Oh, hello everyone.

FRED. What you been doing?

JUDY. Just...getting ready.

FRED. Getting ready? You look as if you've been through a combine harvester!

JUDY. Oh, well, I er....didn't have time really.

FRED. Where's Shaun?

JUDY. *(innocently)* Isn't he here?

FRED. Does it look like he's here? He went to get you.

JUDY. Oh, I must have been in the bathroom.

FRED. It's getting well used that bathroom.

JUDY. *(awkward laugh)* Oo, champagne! Lovely.

(MAURICE brings a tray downstage with the champagne bottle and glasses.)

MAURICE. We all drink a toast now to a wonderful holiday.

(SHAUN enters, also straightening himself.)

SHAUN. Ah, there you all are. Did I just hear the joyful sound of corks popping?

MOIRA. Where've you been, Shaun?

SHAUN. Me? Er...in the bathroom.

FRED. What is it about that bloody bathroom?

SHAUN. I was just, er...

FRED. Were you all in there together or something?

SHAUN. Ah, well – it's the well known Murphy's bathroom law, you see. The more people waiting to go in, the hotter the water gets and the quicker the toilet flushes.

FRED. Eh? What you talking about?

SHAUN. I've no idea.

MOIRA. Well listen, we're not going out tonight after all, Shaun. We're all having dinner here now – courtesy of Maurice and Yvette.

SHAUN. Oh, good – that's great!

FRED. You knew that already.

SHAUN. Yes, so I did. I'd...forgotten.

FRED. Everyone's acting very peculiar round here.

YVETTE. Don't worry so much, Fred. You're on holiday – relax.

FRED. Must be the climate.

YVETTE. *(coming and taking his arm)* Yes. It's Provence. It does strange things to people.

FRED. Does it?

YVETTE. Oh yes. It takes away all their, er...inhibitions. *(flirtatious)* You know what I mean?

FRED. Does it?

YVETTE. You must learn to lose yours, too.

FRED. *(laughing awkwardly)* Not in front of your husband, Yvette.

YVETTE. Oh, we leave him with his philosophies. Some people have better things to do, no?

SHAUN. Oh ho. There you go, Fred. You said you wanted some action this holiday.

FRED. Yeh, but not...I mean...Sorry, Maurice.

MAURICE. Ah, be my guest. Yvette, she is all talk. She just tries to provoke me.

YVETTE. Yes, darling.

(MAURICE hands round glasses.)

MAURICE. Now – champagne!

FRED. *(grabbing a glass with relief)* Oh, cheers.

MAURICE. Sante everyone. We drink to love. We drink to...
   Provence!

ALL. To Provence!

JUDY. And vive la France!

ALL. Vive la France!

MAURICE. Toast, Yvette!

YVETTE. *(twirling)* Vive la difference!

ALL. La difference!

   *(**MAURICE** gestures to **MOIRA**.)*

MOIRA. To...French men!

ALL. French men!

   *(He gestures to **FRED**.)*

FRED. French women!

ALL. French women!

   *(to **SHAUN**)*

SHAUN. French letters!

ALL. Shaun!

   (blackout)

   (curtain)

ACT TWO

Scene One

(A few hours later. Moonlit evening. The six are all seated on the terrace on garden chairs set round a table in front of the patio couch. The remains of the dinner lie on the table, and several empty bottles. Much laughter and ribaldry.)

SHAUN. …and the farmer says, 'well, that bull serviced the cow over three hundred times last year. I don't know how he does it.' And the other man says, 'Was it the same cow three hundred times, or was it three hundred different cows?' And he says, 'Oh, three hundred different cows of course.' 'Ah, well,' says the other fella, 'that's the secret.'

(riotous laughter)

FRED. Same old Shaun.

JUDY. Fred'd love to service three hundred cows a year – wouldn't you, sweetheart?

FRED. Me? Just one cow three times a year would be nice.

(laughter and mockery)

JUDY. Fred! Well maybe you need to learn how to woo cows a bit better, eh?

MOIRA. It's true, Fred – the female sex needs to be wooed.

JUDY. Exactly.

MOIRA. A bit of romance, a bit of flattery. Eh, Maurice?

MAURICE. Oh, yes.

MOIRA. Which is what the French are good at.

YVETTE. Hah!

SHAUN. You don't think so, Yvette?

47

YVETTE. The French bull, he is all talk.

JUDY. Oo!

YVETTE. He woos until he gets what he wants, then he has no more interest.

(chorus of hoots)

SHAUN. There, Maurice. French bulls are all bull.

MOIRA. (stroking MAURICE) Is that true, Maurice? Is it all just surface charm?

MAURICE. It depends on the cow.

(chorus)

YVETTE. Well, some cows get sick of the same tired old bull.

JUDY. Hear, hear!

(chorus)

FRED. Right. So now we all know where we stand, eh?

SHAUN. Well, this tired old bull is going to sober up in the pool. Who's for a skinny dip?

(cheers and hoots)

YVETTE. Skinny dip?

MOIRA. No costumes, Yvette.

YVETTE. Ah.

MAURICE. There is a rule of the house here anyway. No swim costumes allowed after nine o'clock.

FRED. It's a bit soon after dinner for swimming.

JUDY. (getting up) Well I'm game. Who's coming?

FRED. You've changed your tune. You were all against it earlier.

JUDY. It's dark now. I don't mind in the dark.

MOIRA. (rising) Nor me – I'll come! Bring some wine!

MAURICE. There's a bar by the pool.

SHAUN. Maurice? Yvette?

MAURICE. Yes!

YVETTE. I clear the table first.

SHAUN. Last one in's a cissy!

(Heads for the pool, followed by the others, whooping and laughing. FRED *hangs back.)*

FRED. I'll give you a hand.

YVETTE. Thank you.

(They start to clear the table and take the stuff to the kitchen area.)

FRED. Great dinner.

YVETTE. Thank you.

FRED. Everyone's a bit drunk.

YVETTE. You don't want to skinny dip?

FRED. Oh, later p'raps. Could be a bit of a squeeze, all six of us in at once – ha, ha.

YVETTE. It seems we have a situation here, no?

FRED. Situation?

YVETTE. Three marriages – all with problems.

FRED. Problems? You think so?

YVETTE. It seems so. You don't think so?

FRED. Don't all marriages have problems?

YVETTE. Do they?

FRED. What about Shaun and Moira? They're all right.

YVETTE. You think so?

FRED. You don't think so?

YVETTE. I don't think so.

FRED. Why?

YVETTE. I think he likes your wife for one thing.

FRED. Shaun?

YVETTE. Yes.

FRED. Likes Judy?

YVETTE. Oh, yes.

FRED. What makes you say that?

YVETTE. I see it. You don't?

FRED. Shaun?

YVETTE. She likes him too, I think.

FRED. Judy? Nah, they're old friends. *(a beat)* You think so?

YVETTE. *(shrugging)* I see the way they look.

FRED. *(astonished)* Shaun and Judy?

YVETTE. You don't think so?

FRED. Judy and Shaun??

YVETTE. It's not so surprising.

> *(pause)*

FRED. *(stunned)* Shaun and Judy??

YVETTE. Old friends. It happens.

FRED. I don't believe it. How d'you know?

YVETTE. I don't. I just watch.

> *(They move the table and stack the patio chairs.)*

FRED. No, no. No!

YVETTE. I'm sorry. Perhaps I shouldn't say this.

FRED. Not Judy and Shaun. *(stops working)* Although….

YVETTE. What?

FRED. They are always keen to go on holiday together.

YVETTE. Ah.

FRED. And they do…

YVETTE. What?

FRED. Seem to keep disappearing at the same time.

YVETTE. You see.

FRED. I don't believe it! We've known them for years!

YVETTE. It's been happening for years?

FRED. No! Not Shaun and Judy!!

YVETTE. *(putting a hand on his arm)* Don't upset yourself. Perhaps it's not true.

FRED. Bloody hell! It could be true. *(looks towards the pool)* And now they're skinny dipping together!

YVETTE. You must have done that before.

FRED. Well, yes but…. I don't believe it – all those holidays we've had together!

YVETTE. Oh dear, I should not have said. Perhaps I'm wrong.

FRED. You could be right. He's a randy old bastard. I just never…I must be stupid!

YVETTE. No…

FRED. Right in front of my eyes!

YVETTE. Don't say anything. It may not be true.

FRED. How do I find out?

YVETTE. Just watch.

FRED. Yeh, right. Shaun and Judy! Bloody hell!

(looks at her)

Well, if it's true…what's sauce for the goose, eh?

YVETTE. Sorry? Goose?

FRED. Old English expression. *(puts an arm round her)* How about we have our own skinny dip, eh?

YVETTE. Ah – now you get romantic, eh?

FRED. I told you I was.

YVETTE. Just because your wife does too?

FRED. Oh, no. I fancied you right from the start.

YVETTE. Yes?

FRED. Oh, yes. That's my kind of woman, I thought. Sparky, passionate.

YVETTE. It's just because I'm French.

FRED. Well, that too. A bit of entente cordiale, as your hubby says. What about you?

YVETTE. Me?

FRED. Could you fancy me?

YVETTE. English rosbif?

FRED. Yeh. Bit of roast beef. Nice and tender and rare.

YVETTE. Are you tender?

FRED. Oh yeh. *(kisses her)* How's that?

YVETTE. That's nice.

(They kiss again.)

FRED. That's very nice.

YVETTE. Sauce with the goose?

FRED. Sauce *for* the goose. Is sauce for the gander. That's me.

YVETTE. Ah. So the gander want to skinny dip now?

FRED. Not just now.

YVETTE. Why not?

FRED. When I skinny dip with you I'd like it to be on our own.

YVETTE. That is not so easy.

FRED. I'm sure we can find a way. Is Maurice, er...?

YVETTE. What?

FRED. Ever likely to be elsewhere?

YVETTE. Perhaps. Perhaps with Moira.

FRED. Moira?

YVETTE. He likes her, I think.

FRED. Moira??

YVETTE. She certainly likes him.

FRED. Nah – that's all talk.

YVETTE. You think so?

FRED. Don't you think so?

YVETTE. Probably.

FRED. Moira and Maurice! Blimey! How would you feel?

YVETTE. I would kill him.

FRED. Yes, well...It couldn't happen anyway.

YVETTE. Why not?

FRED. How could they? When could they?

YVETTE. If Shaun is somewhere with your wife...

FRED. What?

YVETTE. And I am with you...

FRED. Bloody hell!! This is a flippin' roundabout!

YVETTE. Don't worry. It doesn't happen yet.

FRED. My God – this holiday's certainly started off at a pace!

YVETTE. Well – you wished some excitement in your life, Fred.

FRED. This could be more than I bargained for.

(There are giggles from off-stage, and JUDY *runs on followed by* SHAUN. *They are wearing large beach towels round themselves.)*

FRED. Well, that was quick.

JUDY. Oh, there you are, Fred. Aren't you swimming?

FRED. I'd be a bit of a wallflower, wouldn't I?

JUDY. What d'you mean?

FRED. Wouldn't want to spoil the party.

JUDY. Don't be daft. It's lovely in.

FRED. Why you out so quick then?

JUDY. Oh, we just…wanted a quick dip.

FRED. Quick dip?

JUDY. Yes.

FRED. Sounds good. Nice in, is it, Shaun?

SHAUN. Oh, yes, lovely.

FRED. The others having a 'quick dip'?

SHAUN. Er…yes.

FRED. Well, isn't that friendly?

JUDY. What's up, Fred?

FRED. Good question that. What's up?

JUDY. *(to* SHAUN*)* He's in a silly mood. I'm going in. I need to wash my hair.

FRED. There you go. Second time today. Cleanest hair in France has Judy.

JUDY. Oh, Fred! It's all chloriny.

(goes off)

SHAUN. Yes, well…I'd better go in too – wash my eye-lashes.

(grins feebly, and follows)

FRED. I must be blind!

YVETTE. It's not sure.

FRED. All those holidays together!

YVETTE. Maybe nothing happens.

FRED. I'll find out – one way or another.

YVETTE. I clean the dishes.

(*Goes to the kitchen area.* **MOIRA** *enters from the pool, wearing a beach robe.*)

MOIRA. Fred.

FRED. Moira.

MOIRA. You not swimming?

FRED. Not just yet. Good fun in the dark, was it?

MOIRA. Very good fun.

FRED. Where's Maurice?

MOIRA. Clearing up the pool.

FRED. Bathroom's busy.

MOIRA. I'll wait a bit.

FRED. Have some wine.

(*pours*)

MOIRA. Just a small one.

FRED. Started off well then.

MOIRA. What?

FRED. The holiday.

MOIRA. Oh, yes. Very well.

FRED. (*handing the glass to her*) How are things – with you and Shaun?

MOIRA. Me and Shaun?

FRED. Yeh.

MOIRA. All right. Why?

FRED. Just wondered.

MOIRA. Same as always. Why not?

FRED. Quite fancy Maurice though, don't you?

MOIRA. Ah well – I'd always fancy a dishy man like that. No harm in it.

FRED. No. Not while you and Shaun are all right.

MOIRA. No.

FRED. D'you ever wonder about him?

MOIRA. Maurice?

FRED. Shaun.

MOIRA. What about him?

FRED. D'you ever wonder if...?

MOIRA. What?

FRED. He's got someone else?

MOIRA. Why d'you ask?

FRED. Just wondered.

MOIRA. No, not Shaun. Although...

FRED. What?

MOIRA. He does go away quite a lot. On the business.

FRED. Does he?

MOIRA. It crosses my mind sometimes. You know what men are.

FRED. Where does he go?

MOIRA. All over. But usually London.

FRED. London?

MOIRA. Yes.

FRED. *(frowning)* Usually London?

MOIRA. At least once a month.

FRED. *London?*

MOIRA. You knew that.

FRED. Yes, but...once a month?

MOIRA. I should think so.

FRED. *(pacing)* Bloody hell!

MOIRA. What's up?

FRED. London! It never occurred to me.

MOIRA. D'you think he has someone?

FRED. I dunno. Do you?

MOIRA. I don't know. Do you?

FRED. Unbelievable!

MOIRA. What? You know something.

FRED. No.

MOIRA. Then what is it?

FRED. It's nothing. But if there was something…you'd know, wouldn't you?

MOIRA. I don't know. I wonder sometimes. Do you wonder?

FRED. About Shaun?

MOIRA. Yes.

FRED. Why should I?

MOIRA. Men talk.

FRED. Not me and Shaun.

MOIRA. Ah. What about you and Judy?

FRED. What about us?

MOIRA. Are you all right?

FRED. Oh, yes.

MOIRA. That's all right then.

FRED. Yeh.

MOIRA. I'm sure we're all all right.

FRED. Yeh. Although….

MOIRA. What?

FRED. Well, I do wonder sometimes.

MOIRA. About Judy?

FRED. Judy and Shaun.

MOIRA. Judy and *Shaun!*

FRED. Shh! Don't you?

MOIRA. Shaun and Judy?

FRED. It's possible.

MOIRA. No! Judy and Shaun??

FRED. We're always on holiday.

MOIRA. Yes, but….

FRED. He comes to London.

MOIRA. I know, but…No. Not Shaun and Judy.

(YVETTE *returns from the kitchen area.*)

FRED. Yvette noticed.

MOIRA. What?

FRED. Shaun and Judy. Didn't you, Yvette?

MOIRA. Did you?

YVETTE. It's nothing. I'm sure it's nothing.

MOIRA. What did you notice?

YVETTE. They are just friends.

MOIRA. D'you know, it could be true.

FRED. You think so?

MOIRA. He's always off to London. They're always keen on the holidays.

FRED. That's what I said.

MOIRA. Oh my Lord! How do we tell?

FRED. Just watch.

MOIRA. Judy and Shaun! Oh my Lord!

(MAURICE comes back from the pool. He also wears a bathrobe.)

MAURICE. Ah! The party continues.

YVETTE. Not so good.

MAURICE. Il y'a un problème?

YVETTE. Peut être. You look after Moira. *(takes FRED by the hand)* Come, Fred. We swim now.

FRED. Oh. Right. *(to MAURICE)* Is it all right?

MAURICE. Of course. There are towels by the pool.

(They go off. MAURICE pours himself some wine. MOIRA is distracted.)

You are all right?

MOIRA. Er…yes. Just thinking about something.

MAURICE. There is a problem?

MOIRA. Oh, no. Well, maybe.

MAURICE. Tell me.

MOIRA. It's nothing.

MAURICE. You have a very nice figure.

MOIRA. You promised not to look.

MAURICE. How can I not look?

MOIRA. Well, thank you.

MAURICE. What is the problem?

MOIRA. It's just...well, me and Fred were wondering....

MAURICE. Yes?

MOIRA. About Shaun and Judy. That's all.

MAURICE. Ah, yes. Shaun and Judy.

MOIRA. You knew?

MAURICE. We just wondered. Yvette and me.

MOIRA. About Shaun and Judy?

MAURICE. Yes.

MOIRA. Oh my Lord! Everyone knows except me!

MAURICE. It may not be true. Have some wine.

(*Pours. They sit on the patio couch.*)

MOIRA. I don't believe it. All these years!

MAURICE. Ah, non. Perhaps just this year.

MOIRA. No. I'm sure it's been going on for years.

MAURICE. You think so?

MOIRA. I knew something was up. I must be blind!

MAURICE. These things happen. It's natural.

MOIRA. Maybe for you Frenchies. We're Catholics.

MAURICE. We are Catholics.

MOIRA. Oh, yes.

MAURICE. What has that to do with it?

MOIRA. Nothing, that's true.

MAURICE. Marriage sometimes gets boring.

MOIRA. Yes.

MAURICE. C'est la vie.

MOIRA. C'est la vie.

(*He puts his arm round her.*)

MAURICE. So now you can be free.

MOIRA. Free?

MAURICE. To have your own...distraction.

MOIRA. Oh, Maurice, I'd love to. Nothing I'd like better
    than to have a bit of French cordon bleu on the side,
    but...

MAURICE. But what?

MOIRA. I'm a well brought-up Irish girl.

MAURICE. That's the trouble. You are too well brought up.

MOIRA. You think so?

MAURICE. The Irish men have all the fun, the women don't have any.

MOIRA. That's very true. We're a suppressed nation.

MAURICE. So – now you are in Europe. You have excuse to unsuppress.

(kisses her)

MOIRA. Oh, that's nice. But it's only because I'm drunk.

MAURICE. Of course.

MOIRA. I wouldn't do this sober.

MAURICE. Of course not.

(kisses her again)

MOIRA. That's very nice.

(He moves to put a hand inside her robe. She rises.)

That bastard! I'll have his guts!

MAURICE. Later. Come here.

MOIRA. I'd love to, Maurice. Perhaps when I know you a bit better.

MAURICE. It's the best way to know me.

MOIRA. I know, but it's hard to concentrate when...Shaun and Judy! How could I have been so blind!

(JUDY enters from the bedrooms, in a dressing gown, her hair still damp. SHAUN follows.)

JUDY. Where is everyone? *(sees them on the terrace)* Oh, there you are.

MOIRA. Here we are.

JUDY. Very friendly.

MOIRA. Yes, well...it's good to be friendly, isn't it?

JUDY. Yes.

MOIRA. We're always friendly with everyone, aren't we, Shaun?

SHAUN. That we are.

MOIRA. I mean, *we've* all been friends for years.

SHAUN. That we have.

MOIRA. And it's always good to make new friends, don't you think, Judy?

JUDY. Yes, it is.

MOIRA. Good. That's all right then. *(pats* **MAURICE** *and drinks her wine with abandon)*

JUDY. You all right, Moira?

MOIRA. I'm fine. I'm terrific! Are you all right?

JUDY. I'm terrific.

MOIRA. Terrific! Isn't Provence wonderful?

JUDY. Lovely.

SHAUN. Superb.

MOIRA. *(stroking* **MAURICE***)* And aren't French people lovely?

SHAUN. Lovely.

JUDY. Really lovely.

MAURICE. Thank you.

MOIRA. I tell you what – I think it's going to be a wonderful holiday!

MAURICE. Wonderful. *(to the others)* Please – have some more wine.

JUDY. I think we've had enough.

SHAUN. Well, just a drop.

(fetches wine for himself and **JUDY***)*

MOIRA. Tell me something, Judy.

JUDY. What's that?

MOIRA. Do you think that, when you're on holiday, the normal rules don't apply?

JUDY. What normal rules?

MOIRA. The rules about other people.

JUDY. Other people?

MOIRA. Having fun with other people.

JUDY. Well, I...I dunno.

(SHAUN *returns with the wine.*)

What do you think, Shaun?

SHAUN. Other people?

MOIRA. Yes.

SHAUN. Depends on the people.

MOIRA. Oh, nice people. People who know each other well.

JUDY. Such as?

MOIRA. Well...such as Fred and Yvette for instance.

JUDY. Fred and Yvette?

MOIRA. They're down by the pool. Skinny dipping.

JUDY. Yes, well....

MOIRA. Or me and Maurice for instance. We've been skinny dipping too.

SHAUN. Well, skinny dipping – that's all right. On holiday.

JUDY. When it's all friends together.

MOIRA. Of course. All good friends together.

SHAUN. You all right, Moira?

MOIRA. I'm fine. I'm terrific. Are you all right, Shaun?

SHAUN. I'm terrific.

MOIRA. And are you all right, Maurice?

MAURICE. I am terrific.

MOIRA. There, you see. Everyone's terrific.

SHAUN. But what did you mean?

MOIRA. When?

SHAUN. About having fun?

MOIRA. What do you think I meant?

SHAUN. I don't know.

MOIRA. Aren't you having fun?

SHAUN. Of course I'm having fun!

MOIRA. Well that's all right then.

SHAUN. But what did you *mean* by having fun?

MOIRA. I meant...Tell them what I meant, Maurice.

MAURICE. I think she meant…having a bit more than fun.

SHAUN. A bit more?

MOIRA. Yes. A bit more.

SHAUN. Ah.

MOIRA. So? Is it all right to have a bit more than fun?

JUDY. It depends how much more.

SHAUN. Yes.

MOIRA. Ah. How much more?

JUDY. Yes.

MOIRA. Yes, it would do. Well, that's that settled. *(raises her glass)* Cheers everybody.

> *(They drink.* **SHAUN** *and* **JUDY** *look vaguely uneasy.* **MOIRA** *gets up.)*

> Now I think it's time I got dressed. Just in case I find myself having too much fun.

> *(goes off to the bedrooms, a little unsteadily)*

SHAUN. *(looking after her)* What was all that about?

JUDY. She's drunk too much.

SHAUN. I know, but….

JUDY. We've all drunk too much. Very nice wine though, Maurice.

MAURICE. Thank you.

SHAUN. Do you know what that was about, Maurice?

MAURICE. *(shrugging)* Perhaps she is wondering.

SHAUN. What about?

MAURICE. The way the world is. I go and dress now. Help yourself to the wine.

> *(goes off to his bedroom)*

SHAUN. Fat lot of help that was. What *was* Moira on about?

JUDY. You don't think she suspects, do you?

SHAUN. I don't see how. We haven't done much.

JUDY. Shaun! We've had two quickies already!

SHAUN. She didn't know anything.

JUDY. She's behaving very strange. And she was all over Maurice.

SHAUN. That's just Moira.

JUDY. Not usually that much.

SHAUN. It's the wine. It's this place.

JUDY. I hope you're right. I hope...

SHAUN. What?

JUDY. She doesn't suspect.

SHAUN. No.

JUDY. I hope Fred doesn't suspect.

SHAUN. Why should he?

JUDY. I dunno. Something's up.

> (FRED and YVETTE come back from the pool wearing bathrobes.)

FRED. Beautiful! That was beautiful!

> (sees the others)

Ah. There you are.

JUDY. That was quick.

FRED. Long enough.

JUDY. Nice was it?

FRED. Beautiful.

YVETTE. Beautiful.

FRED. I thought you were washing your hair.

JUDY. I just haven't dried it yet.

FRED. Ah. Better things to do, eh?

JUDY. What?

FRED. Than drying hair and stuff.

JUDY. Oh, yes.

FRED. Whilst on holiday.

JUDY. What d'you mean?

FRED. Nothing. I didn't mean anything.

JUDY. Oh.

YVETTE. You like some wine, Fred?

FRED. I think I've had enough, Yvette. I think we've all had enough. Don't you, Shaun?

SHAUN. Probably.

FRED. I mean enough is enough, isn't it? When you're all together...in the altogether – ha, ha.

SHAUN. What d'you mean, Fred?

FRED. Nothing. Just that. If you've had enough, then it's enough...and we've all had enough...so that's enough. Don't you think?

SHAUN. Yeh.

FRED. Right. Well, I'm going to get dressed. How about you, Yvette?

YVETTE. Yes.

FRED. Time we all got dressed. Unless of course it's bedtime. In which case we should all get undressed – ha, ha.

(goes unsteadily off)

YVETTE. He is a little drunk, I think.

JUDY. Yes.

YVETTE. I think perhaps it's bedtime.

SHAUN. Yes.

YVETTE. I go too. Good night.

JUDY. 'Night.

SHAUN. 'Night.

*(**YVETTE** goes off.)*

JUDY. D'you think he knows?

SHAUN. I don't know.

JUDY. He's acting very strangely.

SHAUN. I don't think he knows.

JUDY. They're both acting strangely.

SHAUN. Perhaps it's just because....

JUDY. What?

SHAUN. Of the others.

JUDY. The Frenchies?

SHAUN. Yes.

JUDY. You think they fancy them?

SHAUN. I think there's quite a lot of fancying going on.

JUDY. We are all drunk.

SHAUN. Yes.

JUDY. But still...they could suspect.

SHAUN. No...Though they might be vaguely wondering.

JUDY. Yes. Just wondering.

SHAUN. *(pacing)* It's difficult.

JUDY. What is?

SHAUN. We don't know if they know, or if they're just wondering. If they know, then they don't know if we know they know, or if we're just wondering. If they're just wondering, then we don't *know* if they're wondering, or whether they know...in which case *we're* just wondering.

(pause)

JUDY. What you talking about?

SHAUN. I've no idea.

JUDY. Well, let's stop wondering until we know, all right? Otherwise we'll go mad.

SHAUN. Right.

JUDY. But we'll have to be very careful.

SHAUN. Yes. *(pause)* So when do we get to do it?

JUDY. Shaun!

SHAUN. I can't go the whole holiday without you.

JUDY. Perhaps we can sneak out at night. Fred sleeps like a log.

SHAUN. Moira's used to me getting up.

JUDY. How do we get out at the same time?

SHAUN. Like usual. Listen for me to flush the toilet.

JUDY. Right.

SHAUN. Now I think we should all go to bed.

JUDY. Yes.

SHAUN. Have a little sleep….

JUDY. Yes.

SHAUN. And see what happens.

JUDY. Right.

(They head for the bedrooms.)

SHAUN. I'll tell you one thing.

JUDY. What?

SHAUN. I'm glad I'm not a bull. Managing three hundred cows would be just too much!

(blackout)

Scene Two

(A couple of hours later. The stage is in darkness. The sound of a toilet flushing. Pause. A shadowy figure emerges from the guest bedrooms. Comes out onto the terrace and sits on the patio couch.)

(Pause. A second figure follows.)

JUDY. *(whispering)* Shaun?

SHAUN. *(ditto)* Over here.

(She creeps out and joins him on the couch.)

JUDY. Oh, Shaun....

SHAUN. Judy....

(Sounds of passion. The patio couch swings. Another shadow appears from the bedrooms. Bumps into the furniture.)

FRED. *(whispering)* Bugger!

(Instant silence from the terrace. FRED creeps to the sofa. A shadow comes out of the main bedroom.)

FRED. *(whispering)* Yvette?

YVETTE. *(ditto)* Fred?

FRED. Over here.

(She closes the bedroom door, sneaks over and joins him on the sofa. Sounds of passion. The bedroom door opens again. Instant silence. A shadow slides out. Another appears from the other side.)

MAURICE. *(whispering)* Moira?

MOIRA. *(ditto)* Maurice?

MAURICE. Here.

(They approach the sofa from opposite sides, and fall onto it. Shrieks and exclamations from all parties. General pandemonium on the sofa. MAURICE gets up and puts on the lights. All six are revealed in their night attire)

MAURICE. Fred!

FRED. Maurice!

YVETTE. Maurice!

MAURICE. Yvette!

FRED. Moira!

MOIRA. Fred!

(MAURICE *sees* SHAUN *and* JUDY *on the patio couch.*)

MAURICE. Oh, la la!

(*The others follow his gaze.*)

FRED. Judy!

JUDY. Fred!

MOIRA. Shaun!

SHAUN. Moira!

(*Pause. They all gather cautiously on the terrace.*)

FRED. Bloody hell! What's going on?

JUDY. Yes – what *is* going on?

MOIRA. Yes, what is going on?

FRED. I asked first.

SHAUN. And I'm asking last.

JUDY. This is ridiculous!

MOIRA. You may call it ridiculous, Judy – that's my husband you're consorting with there.

JUDY. Consorting with! What's that supposed to mean?

FRED. It's very obvious what it means!

SHAUN. Have you tried consorting on a swing-sofa?

MOIRA. Don't you try and joke your way out of this, Shaun!

SHAUN. All right, what were you two doing with those two? Is it called something different in French?

JUDY. It's not called consorting, that's for sure.

SHAUN. Cavorting more like.

FRED. Oh, don't you get moralistic with us!

MOIRA. What we're doing is not remotely comparable to what you're doing!

JUDY. Why? Do you do it differently to us?

FRED. We don't do it as often, it seems! How long's this been going on?

JUDY. How long's what been going on?

MOIRA. You know what he's talking about!

SHAUN. I don't know at all what he's talking about. *(pointing at FRED and YVETTE)* How long's *this* been going on?

MOIRA. About three hours, that's how long.

FRED. And nothing much is going on anyway!

JUDY. Didn't look like nothing much to us!

MOIRA. Well, it's nothing much compared to what's been going on with you.

SHAUN. How do you know what's been going on with us?

FRED. It's pretty obvious what's been going on with you!

MOIRA. And for a lot longer than three hours!

JUDY. Oh, I see – so doing it in double quick time with a French poodle makes it all all right, does it?

YVETTE. A what?

FRED. Better than doing it every month with an Irish bull.

JUDY. Now look here....!

MOIRA. Who doesn't care how many cows he has!

SHAUN. Now you look here....!

(All four start shouting and gesticulating at once. It is rapidly turning into a brawl when MAURICE puts his fingers to his mouth and gives an ear-splitting whistle. Silence)

MAURICE. *(gently)* If you don't mind me saying so, this is a little undignified.

FRED. Oh, pardon, monsieur, let's be dignified by all means.

MAURICE. Is this how the British conduct their arguments?

SHAUN. Well maybe this situation is so common in France that you don't have arguments about it, but it's a little different with us.

YVETTE. No. It is a difficult situation for all of us, but Maurice is right. We should discuss it in a civilised way.

MAURICE. Exactly.

FRED. Civilised?

MAURICE. Yes.

FRED. All right, let's do that. You start.

MAURICE. Moi?

FRED. You want a civilised discussion. Let's discuss what you were doing meeting up with Shaun's wife at two in the morning in your pyjamas.

SHAUN. Quite.

MAURICE. It's obvious.

FRED. It is?

MAURICE. I am doing the same as he is doing with your wife, and you are doing with my wife. We are all meeting for a little romance, a little affection to relieve the monotony of our marriages. No?

FRED. Well...

MAURICE. And where better to do it than in Provence, on a summer's night, after a good dinner with too much wine?

FRED. Yes, well....put like that....

YVETTE. Of course. He would always put it like that.

MOIRA. Now wait a minute. We're not letting it go as simply as that.

MAURICE. Why not?

MOIRA. There's a lot more to this than some harmless holiday game.

FRED. Yes, quite.

MOIRA. Correct me if I'm wrong, Judy, but isn't it a fact that you've been having an affair with my husband on a regular basis, both on holiday and in London, for more years than I'd care to count?

JUDY. What makes you think that?

MOIRA. Are you denying it?

JUDY. Er...well...I, er....

MOIRA. Thank you, that's all the answer I need. And also isn't it a fact that all I've done with Maurice is have a quick kiss on the sofa, and a sneaky look at his naughty bits by the swimming pool. Likewise Fred and Yvette. Which isn't the same thing in any way whatsoever.

SHAUN. Now hold on here...

MOIRA. Yes, Shaun? Have you something to say on the matter?

SHAUN. Yes, I have....

MOIRA. If it's a joke I'll brain you!

SHAUN. Don't tell either of us that if either of you had been here on your own with either of them, you wouldn't have done a good deal more than a quick kiss on the sofa.

JUDY. Exactly.

SHAUN. Don't tell us that, if we hadn't all interrupted each other at the same time just now, the amount of serious bonking going on here would not have reached epic proportions. In which case, since the intention is as good as the act, there's absolutely no difference between any of us.

FRED. You what??

SHAUN. What?

FRED. Are you seriously claiming that a long-standing affair with another man's wife is the same as a hypothetical, theoretical one-night stand on holiday with someone you've never met before?

YVETTE. A one-night stand? Oh thank you, is that all I was going to be?

FRED. No, no, of course not, but...

JUDY. There you are, you see! You were hell-bent on starting a full scale ding-dong, same as everyone else. You can't get all self-righteous with us.

FRED. Well, maybe I wouldn't have wanted a full-scale ding-dong if I'd been getting what I wanted at home. But since you were giving it all to Shaun all this time it's not surprising I went looking elsewhere.

JUDY. Oh, I see – it's *my* fault now you've gone and entered the Common Market!

FRED. Well…

JUDY. And I suppose it's Shaun's fault that Moira's applied for membership too?

SHAUN. Is that right? Is that what you're saying, Moira?

MOIRA. She said that, I never said that. But is that what you're saying about me?

SHAUN. Well, I'm not saying quite that, but er….

MOIRA. *(to JUDY)* Is that what you're saying about Fred?

JUDY. Me? I, er…well I don't know, I….

MOIRA. Maurice, are you saying about Yvette what Fred's saying about Judy and Shaun's saying about me?

MAURICE. I don't know – I've lost the meaning of this conversation.

MOIRA. Well, it seems to me that everyone's got a lot to say about everyone else, and everyone else has got some excuse for what they're doing with everyone else, but no-one's going to get very far going round and round in circles like this.

SHAUN. So what do you suggest?

MOIRA. I suggest that the best thing is for everyone to simmer down now, go back to bed, and we'll discuss it all in the morning.

FRED. Hang on – I've got some more questions to ask first.

MOIRA. The trouble with asking questions, Fred, is you might have to answer some yourself.

FRED. That's all right – *I* don't mind answering questions!

YVETTE. Are you sure, Mr. Gander?

JUDY. *(frowning)* Who?

FRED. Yeh…well, I er….

MOIRA. Perhaps you'd rather do it dressed, sober, and in the daylight, Fred.

FRED. *(grudging)* Yes, well…all right.

MOIRA. Is everyone agreed? *(silence)* I'll take that as a yes. So – no more discussions and no more nocturnal expeditions. See you all at breakfast. Goodnight.

(Everyone drifts back to their respective bedrooms. Not without the odd petulant mutter, and an occasional push and slap between spouses.)

(The lights dim.)

Scene Three

(Next morning. Bright sunshine. The setting has not changed. **YVETTE** *comes out of the main bedroom dressed in natty beach shorts and top. She carries two bathrobes which she lays on the sofa ready for the pool. She goes to the kitchen area, puts on the kettle, and starts to set out a bowl of fruit and cut up bread, etc.* **MAURICE** *comes out in shorts and summer shirt. They barely glance at one another. He collects dirty glasses from the night before, and takes them to the kitchen.)*

MAURICE. *(dour)* Excusez moi.

*(***FRED*** comes blearily out from the other side. They all glance at each other, and* **MAURICE** *passes him to collect more glasses.)*

MAURICE. Excuse me.

*(***FRED*** comes downstage to the terrace and sits on the patio couch.* **JUDY** *comes out.* **MAURICE** *passes her as he returns to the kitchen.)*

MAURICE. Excuse me.

*(***JUDY*** heads for the terrace. Sees* **FRED** *and stops. Turns and sits on the sofa.* **SHAUN** *comes out. Sees the Frenchies.)*

SHAUN. Excuse me.

(Turns to the sofa, sees **JUDY***, heads for the terrace, sees* **FRED***, goes to the other side and stares out front.* **MOIRA** *comes out. Sees everyone, and goes to the other end of the sofa from* **JUDY***.)*

MOIRA. *(sitting, to* **JUDY***)* Excuse me.

*(***JUDY*** moves up.* **MAURICE** *comes out to the terrace and sets up the table in front of* **FRED***.)*

MAURICE. Excuse me.

*(***FRED*** moves his legs.* **MAURICE** *puts up the garden chairs.* **YVETTE** *brings the breakfast down to the table.)*

YVETTE. Excuse me.

(Sets out the table as **FRED** *watches. She turns to everyone.)*

Breakfast.

(Sits and helps herself to some fruit. Everyone comes down to the terrace and sits in silence. They help themselves.)

ALL. *(together)* Well, I think...It's time we...I feel we... *(etc.)*

(All stop. Silence. All start again. Silence.)

MAURICE. O.K. I will be the chairman. I think...

SHAUN. Why should you be chairman?

JUDY. Why shouldn't he be chairman?

MAURICE. *(to* **SHAUN***)* You want to be the chairman?

SHAUN. No.

MAURICE. Anyone else want to be the chairman?

MOIRA. Chair person, please.

MAURICE. Whatever.

ALL. *(together)* No.

MAURICE. O.K. I be the chairman. I think we take it in turns. We stand up and we all say what we feel about the situation. *(protests)* No interruptions! When someone speaks. Questions only at the end. Yes?

(reluctant murmurs and nods)

Judy, you go first.

JUDY. Why me?

MAURICE. Why not?

JUDY. Oh no, I'm not going first.

*(***MAURICE*** sighs.)*

MAURICE. Very well.

(hands round the bread basket)

Everyone close their eyes, take a piece of bread.

FRED. What for?

MAURICE. Because I am the chairman. Take a piece of bread.

(Everyone does so.)

Put your bread in front, like this.

(Places his bread on the table in front of him. All copy.)

The biggest goes first, the smallest last. *(scans the bread)* Moira – you're first.

MOIRA. *(pointing at FRED's)* His is bigger than mine!

FRED. No, it's not.

MOIRA. Yes it is – look....

MAURICE. I am the chairman! Yours is the biggest.

MOIRA. *(ungraciously)* This is silly.

FRED. Come on, Moira. Speak up.

MOIRA. What do I say?

MAURICE. Explain how you feel.

MOIRA. Angry.

MAURICE. Everyone feels angry. Tell why you think you should be more angry than everyone else.

MOIRA. All right. *(diffidently)* Well...

MAURICE. *(gesturing)* Stand up.

MOIRA: *(standing awkwardly)* I admit I was flirting with Maurice...

SHAUN. Flirting – hah!

MAURICE. Silence!

MOIRA. He's an attractive man, and we're on holiday, and I was drunk, and...well...But that's all it was...well, all it would have been...if I hadn't found out about my husband and Judy. So.

(pause)

MAURICE. Is that all? Is that it?

MOIRA. Yes. I was very angry. So – I wanted to get my own back.

YVETTE. I understand this.

MAURICE. No comments please! Questions?

FRED. Well you did find out about Shaun and Judy. So would you have let it have go further?

MOIRA. Well...

FRED. Well?

MOIRA. I might have.

SHAUN. Might have?

MOIRA. Well...I never have before...but you've apparently been doing it for years...and, thinking about it, I've been suspicious for years...and I've been wondering myself what it would be like for years...and Maurice is the most attractive man I've met for years...so...

YVETTE. So maybe you make up for all the years.

MOIRA. Well...maybe. Sorry, Yvette.

YVETTE. *(shrugging)* C'est la vie.

MAURICE. Thank you, I am flattered.

SHAUN. *(to MAURICE)* Don't get carried away now!

MAURICE. Next one. *(looks at the bread)* Fred.

FRED. Oh Lord! Yes, well....

MAURICE. Stand up.

FRED. *(standing)* Same as Moira really. I mean, when it's in the air, and it's all around, and you haven't been getting much of it, and everybody else is getting it, then I suppose...you'll grab it wherever you can get it.

YVETTE. Thank you very much.

FRED. No, no – I didn't mean...I mean you're the sexiest woman I've met in a long time, Yvette, and when the opportunity's there...I don't know if it was there...but if it *had* been there...I suppose I might have...

SHAUN. Done it there.

FRED. Well...maybe.

SHAUN. No maybe about it.

MOIRA. Don't judge everyone by your standards, Shaun!

MAURICE. Right. Questions?

JUDY. Yes. *(to YVETTE)* Was the opportunity there?

MAURICE. Ah, no. This is for when her turn comes. *(looks at the bread)* Who is next biggest?

SHAUN. This is like being in the showers at school.

FRED. Belt up, Shaun!

MAURICE. Judy.

JUDY. Gawd! Well...how can I say?

MAURICE. Tell the truth. All the truth.

JUDY. All right... *(*MAURICE *gestures. She stands.)* I've been having a ding-dong with Shaun. I know I shouldn't. *(to* FRED*)* I don't love him. But he gives me excitement. He gives me romance. He gives me fun. And we don't have much of that in our marriage. So there it is.

FRED. That's it?

JUDY. Yes.

FRED. All this time, all these holidays, you two have been at it like rabbits, and all because he gives you *fun?*

JUDY. Yes.

FRED. And I don't?

JUDY. No.

FRED. I don't give you excitement?

JUDY. No.

YVETTE. He doesn't give you romance?

JUDY. No.

MOIRA. And Shaun gives you all these things?

JUDY. Yes.

MOIRA. Holy Mother! Where d'you get all that from, Shaun?

SHAUN. *(shrugging)* Don't ask me.

FRED. Don't ask me either. Bloody hell!

MAURICE. Any questions for Judy?

   (silence)

   Well, you are next Shaun. So you can tell us where you get it from.

SHAUN. I don't know. I've never been a very exciting, romantic sort of person. But Judy makes me feel that way, so....

FRED. You've always been sex-mad!

SHAUN. Not really. It's all talk. But with her it's different.

(*pause*)

MOIRA. Is that all?

SHAUN. Yes.

MOIRA. It's different?

SHAUN. Yes.

FRED. How is it different?

SHAUN. Well...like she says, it's...different.

MAURICE. Is this all the Irish have to say about sex?

SHAUN. I could tell a joke.

ALL. No, thank you!

MAURICE. So. Next. Yvette.

YVETTE. Ah, mon dieu. O.K. – I don't really fancy Fred. He's a nice man, but...not for me. Sorry, Fred. I just try to make my husband jealous.

FRED. Oh, great.

YVETTE. Because I think he is bored with me. Like all French husbands. I think he makes love to all the women he meets. So...I fight the French way.

MAURICE. Which women I make love to?

YVETTE. Michelle...

MAURICE. Non!

YVETTE. Marie-Claire....

MAURICE. Non!

YVETTE. Danielle....

MAURICE. Non!

YVETTE. Tous!

MAURICE. Ah – Yvette!

FRED. Blimey, Maurice – that's going it.

MAURICE. It's not true! She imagines.

YVETTE. I don't imagine with Moira.

MAURICE. Like Moira says, it was flirting.

YVETTE. More than flirting. Moira said she might go all the way. If she does, do you?

MAURICE. Ah… *(hesitates)*

JUDY. Answer the question, Maurice.

MAURICE. *(shrugging)* Is there any man here who could say no to an attractive woman like that?

YVETTE. There it is!

MAURICE. C'est la vie.

SHAUN. That seems to be the answer to everything round here.

FRED. So now what?

MAURICE. Now what what?

FRED. Where does that leave us? We all know why we've been having it off, or trying to have it off, or failing to have it off – and we all feel equally pissed off – so what do we do next?

MOIRA. I'll tell you what we do next.

SHAUN. What?

MOIRA. How do you feel about me, Fred?

FRED. What do you mean?

MOIRA. As a woman. Could you ever find me vaguely attractive?

FRED. Attractive?

MOIRA. Sexy.

FRED. Of course. I've always thought you were lovely, Moira, but…

MOIRA. Well then…I can't answer for Yvette and Maurice here – they have to find their own solutions. But it seems to me that amongst us four there's only one way to put things right. Shaun and Judy have been working out their frustrations together. At our expense. So you and I should do the same.

FRED. You what?

MOIRA. I think you and I should go off to Cannes, Saint Tropez or somewhere, find a nice romantic hotel for a night…or maybe two…and have a bit of that fun and excitement that everyone else is so hell-bent in getting.

SHAUN. Just a minute now....

MOIRA. Quiet, Shaun, you've no rights in this matter.

FRED. D'you mean....?

MOIRA. I mean we should go off and shag each other silly.

JUDY. I beg your pardon!!

MOIRA. Yes, Judy? Do you have a moral objection to that?

JUDY. Yes, I bloody well do! Just because Shaun and I...just because we....

MOIRA. Just because you've found reason to break all the rules, it doesn't mean anyone else has the right to?

JUDY. Well not like that...I mean, not in cold blood at the drop of a hat.

MOIRA. Oh, it would be quite hot-blooded, I promise you that. And when you think about it, it's a very good way of leveling the scales, isn't it? Or can you think of another way?

JUDY. Well, I... *(turns to* **SHAUN***)* Shaun! Say something!

SHAUN. Holy Mother! I don't know....

MOIRA. What do you say, Fred?

FRED. Bloody hell!

MOIRA. From what I gather, you're pretty desperate for a bit of real female warmth and passion. Well I'm offering it to you. And Judy has no possible right to object.

FRED. Blimey!

MAURICE. This sounds like a very good solution to me.

SHAUN. *(aggressively)* Who asked you?

MAURICE. Sorry.

MOIRA. Fred?

FRED. I'm thinking.

JUDY. Fred!

FRED. *(to* **JUDY***)* Let me ask you something.

JUDY. What?

FRED. How many times have you and Shaun done it already since we've been here?

JUDY. Oh, Fred....

FRED. Come on – the truth.

JUDY. *(reluctant)* Twice.

FRED. Christ! You don't hang about, do you?

SHAUN. Oh now, Fred....

FRED. Shut up you! *(to* **MOIRA***)* Yes. Right. I'm on.

JUDY. Fred!

FRED. I said I was going to roger something this holiday. Moira will do very nicely, thank you. *(takes* **MOIRA** *by the hand and heads towards the bedrooms)* Come on, Moira, let's go and pack.

MOIRA. Right.

SHAUN. *(stopping him)* Now, just a minute!

FRED. Out of my way, Shaun.

SHAUN. No, I won't get out of your way! If you think I'm going to let you waltz off to Cannes with my wife...

FRED. Why not? You've been waltzing around Clapham with mine!

SHAUN. *(pushing him back)* That's different...

FRED. *(pushing back)* How is it different?

SHAUN. We seriously fancy each other. We....

FRED. *We* fancy each other. In fact I'm beginning to realise I've fancied Moira rotten for years! Don't know why it took me so long to see it.

SHAUN. *(pushing him)* You're not going!

FRED. *(pushing back)* I bloody am going!

SHAUN. Over my dead body!

FRED. That can be arranged!

(They start wildly brawling, throwing badly aimed punches, ineffectual karate kicks, wrestling and slapping. The women scream at them to stop. **MAURICE** *comes forward and parts them.)*

MAURICE. Non! Stop! STOP!

(They stop and glower at each other, panting.)

Enough. This is stupid.

JUDY. Yes – plain stupid! *(slaps* FRED*)* You're like a couple of schoolboys!

MOIRA. It was quite exciting though.

JUDY. Eh?

MOIRA. I've never had anybody fight over me before. Thank you, Fred. Thank you, Shaun.

SHAUN. What do you mean, thank you?

MOIRA. That's all I wanted to see. We'll call off the pretence now.

SHAUN. Pretence?

MOIRA. I never had any real intention of going off with Fred. No offence, Fred.

FRED. What?

MOIRA. I just wanted to see if my darling husband cared even remotely enough about me to put up a fight. And he did. A pretty laughable fight admittedly, but a fight. And so I think I can just about find a way of forgiving him for what's happened – provided he and Judy agree that the whole thing ends here and now – for good.

JUDY. What?

MOIRA. You heard me.

FRED. You mean, that's it? No going off to Cannes?

MOIRA. I'm sorry, Fred. It would have been nice – but not really very healthy for our marriages when you think about it. I just wanted to see how Shaun would react.

FRED. Bloody hell – missed out again!

SHAUN. *(to* FRED*)* Hah!

FRED. Don't you...!

(Launches into SHAUN. *The fight begins again.* MAU-RICE *pulls them apart.)*

MAURICE. Non! Non!

FRED. All right, all right.

(They calm down.)

Well, now what?

YVETTE. C'est impossible!

MAURICE. Quoi?

YVETTE. This is impossible situation. I think I go back to Paris.

MAURICE. Ah no, Yvette!

ALL. No, Yvette...! You can't do that...! You mustn't go...! *(etc.)*

YVETTE. *(shrugging)* What can we do? C'est trop difficile. Leave them the house. Let them fight together. Better we go back and take the holiday another time.

MAURICE. Attend, Yvette. Ce n'est pas fini.

> *(turns to SHAUN)*
>
> Shaun...

SHAUN. What?

MAURICE. You wish to save the holiday?

SHAUN. Of course.

MAURICE. Then you agree now it's finished with Judy?

SHAUN. *(hesitating)* Well...

FRED. WELL??

SHAUN. *(reluctantly)* All right.

MAURICE. Judy?

JUDY. *(reluctantly)* Yes.

MAURICE. You all agree now we should try a little French romance with our own partners?

YVETTE. Hah!

MAURICE. We too. We all try to mend things. No more fights. No more skinny dips with the wrong persons. No more – how you say – rogers in secret. *(to the men)* All right?

SHAUN. All right.

FRED. All right.

> *(He turns to the girls.)*

JUDY. All right.

YVETTE. Right.

MAURICE. Right. Yvette – we go for our morning swim now. We leave these people to decide how they save the situation.

YVETTE. I don't know...

MAURICE. Yes, you do. Because I tell you.

(He picks up the bathrobes. Turns to them all.)

Provence waits for you. Do not waste it.

(Takes YVETTE *by the hand and leads her off to the pool. The others stand around awkwardly.)*

FRED. So what now?

SHAUN. I don't know.

FRED. Bloody hell!

*(*MOIRA *draws* JUDY *aside and whispers in her ear.)*

What are you two up to?

MOIRA. Shh! *(carries on whispering)*

SHAUN. What are they up to?

FRED. I dunno.

(pause)

You sod!

SHAUN. Yeh.

FRED. Just can't keep it in your trousers, can you?

SHAUN. No.

FRED. You're a sod.

SHAUN. Yeh.

JUDY. *(to* MOIRA*)* Yes. I agree.

FRED. What?

SHAUN. What?

(The women return to them.)

JUDY. Moira and I feel we shouldn't stay here.

SHAUN. What?

FRED. What d'you mean?

MOIRA. We've sabotaged the Frenchies' holiday enough. And our own.

JUDY. We ought to start again.

SHAUN. Start again?

MOIRA. We think we should all go off to a hotel together. Perhaps not Cannes – perhaps some nice little auberge in the countryside. We ought to leave them in peace, and go and try to sort things out on our own. What do you say?

FRED. Well…I don't know.

SHAUN. I'm not sure.

FRED. This place took a lot of finding.

JUDY. Well, while you're thinking about it, we'll go and pack. Come on, Moira.

(The girls go off to the bedrooms.)

SHAUN. What do you think?

FRED. We've paid a lot of dosh for this place. D'you think we could ask for a refund?

SHAUN. No.

FRED. No. Well, I suppose it's not a bad idea.

SHAUN. Yes. It wouldn't be right to stay here now. Not after you and Moira tried to screw them both.

FRED. Now look here!

SHAUN. Sorry, sorry! I withdraw that.

(pause)

FRED. *(sighing)* We've made a right balls-up of this trip, haven't we?

SHAUN. And it's only just started.

FRED. Well, maybe we can save something.

SHAUN. There's some beautiful places in the mountains.

FRED. Should be some vacancies away from the coast.

SHAUN. It's cheaper there.

FRED. Some nice little restaurants.

SHAUN. Very dishy young waitresses, some of them have.

FRED. Shut up, Shaun!

SHAUN. Sorry.

FRED. You only fancy your wife from now on.

SHAUN. I'll try. *(a beat)* It is against human nature though.

FRED. Yes, well...

SHAUN. It's a very bad system.

FRED. Blame God for that.

SHAUN. Ah, no. I'm a Catholic.

FRED. What's that got to do with it?

SHAUN. Nothing.

FRED. Seems to me your first port of call should be the local priest and a very long confession.

SHAUN. Yes.

(The girls return with the suitcases.)

MOIRA. Ready, boys?

FRED. That was quick.

JUDY. We want to settle it before they come back. If we're all agreed, get these in the car.

FRED. Yeh – right.

SHAUN. Right.

FRED. *(picking up the cases)* Gawd, what do they put in these?

SHAUN. Don't ask me.

FRED. *(taking the cases out)* You're a sod!

SHAUN. Yeh.

(They leave. JUDY comes to the terrace and looks towards the pool.)

JUDY. Are we going to say goodbye?

MOIRA. No. Let's just get out. I'll leave them a note.

(She looks for a pen and paper, and scribbles.)

JUDY. *(looking round the room)* Pity. Lovely place. I never even got to use that nice kitchen.

MOIRA. Take a tip, Judy – forget about kitchens for a couple of weeks.

JUDY. Right.

MOIRA. You're a silly tart, you know.

JUDY. Yeh.

(MOIRA leaves the note in a prominent place. Comes downstage and looks at the view. Sighs.)

MOIRA. Beautiful.

JUDY. Yeh.

MOIRA. Pity.

JUDY. Yeh.

MOIRA. *(looking towards the pool)* They're coming back, I think. Let's go. *(at the door)* Silly tart!

JUDY. Yeh.

(They leave, closing the door quietly. Car doors slam. Sound of the car driving off. Pause. MAURICE and YVETTE return, in their bathrobes.)

MAURICE. Hello? *(silence)* Hello?

YVETTE. *(looking out of the rear window)* La voiture n'est pas là.

(MAURICE goes off to the bedrooms.)

MAURICE. *(off)* Ils sont partis!

YVETTE. Eh, bien…

(Sees the note and picks it up. MAURICE returns.)

YVETTE. *(reading)* 'Goodbye Frenchies. Enjoy your holiday. Toujours l'amour, and vive la France!'

MAURICE. Eh. *(grins at her)* It has worked. We lost them.

YVETTE. Très bien.

(He comes downstage and gazes out over the view.)

MAURICE. Strange people, uh?

YVETTE. *(joining him)* Oui.

MAURICE. They never fit in Europe.

YVETTE. Non….

(He puts his arm round her.)

MAURICE. C'est la vie.

YVETTE. C'est la vie.

(The lights dim slowly.)

Curtain

From the Reviews of
A NIGHT IN PROVENCE...

"...Now this admirable dinner theatre is reducing audiences to helpless laughter once more with this consistently entertaining playwright's latest work...makes for a great night out."
-Oxford Times

"Chaos, banter, and sexually charged jokes ensue when three couples clash at a holiday villa in Provence...This fast-paced romp was a joy to watch from start to finish...A wonderful way to spice up a chilly evening."
-Wokingham Times

"An overcrowded French holiday villa makes for a houseful of laughs...Robin Hawdon keeps the sexual frisson simmering in one of the Mill's unqualified successes..."
-Reading Evening Post

"...The audience's delight at the unpredictable final scene indicates the ultimate success of this fast moving comedy...A thoroughly enjoyable evening at the theatre."
-Henley Standard

"Robin Hawdon's latest comedy is ideal fare to cheer us up now the darker nights are here...The sparkling dialogue is guaranteed to ensure the peals of laughter will last through to the end of the run."
-Reading Chronicle

"There is nothing quite like a frothy, amusing tale to send you out of the theatre feeling good, and Robin Hawdon's new comedy does just that. Inspired by the pros and cons of the European Union... nothing short of brilliant...bringing together three couples sharing a glamourous location overlooking the sea...where sun, wine, and skinny dipping under the moon has its effect."
-The Stage

TREASURE ISLAND
Ken Ludwig

All Groups / Adventure / 10m, 1f (doubling) / Areas

Based on the masterful adventure novel by Robert Louis Stevenson, *Treasure Island* is a stunning yarn of piracy on the tropical seas. It begins at an inn on the Devon coast of England in 1775 and quickly becomes an unforgettable tale of treachery and mayhem featuring a host of legendary swashbucklers including the dangerous Billy Bones (played unforgettably in the movies by Lionel Barrymore), the sinister two-timing Israel Hands, the brassy woman pirate Anne Bonney, and the hideous form of evil incarnate, Blind Pew. At the center of it all are Jim Hawkins, a 14-year-old boy who longs for adventure, and the infamous Long John Silver, who is a complex study of good and evil, perhaps the most famous hero-villain of all time. Silver is an unscrupulous buccaneer-rogue whose greedy quest for gold, coupled with his affection for Jim, cannot help but win the heart of every soul who has ever longed for romance, treasure and adventure.

THE OFFICE PLAYS
Two full length plays by Adam Bock

THE RECEPTIONIST
Comedy / 2m., 2f. Interior

At the start of a typical day in the Northeast Office, Beverly deals effortlessly with ringing phones and her colleague's romantic troubles. But the appearance of a charming rep from the Central Office disrupts the friendly routine. And as the true nature of the company's business becomes apparent, The Receptionist raises disquieting, provocative questions about the consequences of complicity with evil.

"...Mr. Bock's poisoned Post-it note of a play."
- New York Times

"Bock's intense initial focus on the routine goes to the heart of
The Receptionist's pointed, painfully timely allegory... elliptical,
provocative play..."
- Time Out New York

THE THUGS
Comedy / 2m, 6f / Interior

The Obie Award winning dark comedy about work, thunder and the mysterious things that are happening on the 9th floor of a big law firm. When a group of temps try to discover the secrets that lurk in the hidden crevices of their workplace, they realize they would rather believe in gossip and rumors than face dangerous realities.

"Bock starts you off giggling, but leaves you with a chill."
- Time Out New York

"... a delightfully paranoid little nightmare that is both more
chillingly realistic and pointedly absurd than anything
John Grisham ever dreamed up."
- New York Times

SAMUELFRENCH.COM